THE SOCAL SLEUTHS

Secret of the Jetty

Rina Torri

Rina TorriCopyright 2020 Rina Torri

Cover photo by Peter Twomey Petertwomey7@gmail.com

ISBN: 978-1-09833-204-4

eBook ISBN: 978-1-09833-205-1

To my daughter
Constant encourager in all my endeavours
every step of the way

Prologue

As Peggy Conti Crawford peered over the edge of the jetty on South Ponto Beach in Carlsbad, her attention was suddenly riveted on one spot.

"Oh, my dear God!" she shouted as she started inching her way down the rocks for a closer look.

"What? What is it?" Barb and Cassie, right behind her, asked in unison as they watched their friend descend.

The body of a woman lying flat in a cradle of rocks was unmistakable. It almost seemed that her skin was metallic so tightly did her soaking wet silver dress cling to every bone and curve. Her long copper blonde hair was splayed out in strands. Her arms were flailed outward, her legs were metal-rod straight.

"I don't think she's alive," Peggy called out. "She looks dead!"

Barb started down the rocks. As soon as she saw the bloated, wrinkled face, limp limbs, closed eyes and slack jaw, she knew the answer to Peggy's question without having to first check for a heartbeat.

"This is horrible. It's too late for resuscitation," Barb realized, having seen more than enough dead patients before retiring from her long career as a nurse practitioner. She also did not have a shred of doubt that the woman had been dead for some time.

"What an awful accident; she must have slipped," said Cassie, gazing down from her perch on an angled rock at the top of the jetty and pulling her cell phone from her waistband.

"I'll call for an ambulance to transport her body to the morgue."

As Cassie stepped to a flatter rock in the center of the jetty, something shiny, adjacent to one of the nearby crevices caught her attention. Bending down, she was dazzled by a shoe that had narrowly escaped falling into the crack and had landed at an angle which allowed the sunlight to play across its metallic-finish surface and create a shimmering spectrum of colors. The sole of the shoe was practically pristine.

This is the most stunning, iridescent shoe I've ever seen, she thought. But what woman in her right mind would ever attempt to wear spike heels on a jetty? What's it doing here and where's the other shoe?

"What do you make of this?" Cassie called down to Peggy and Barb as she held the shoe up high by its skinny long heel. "I don't see the other shoe anywhere."

Peggy stared at the shoe, then back at Cassie, with an expression of horror.

"The other shoe is not missing; it's on this woman's foot. Don't call for an ambulance, call the police.

"This was not an accident. This was murder!"

1

FRIDAY NIGHT, OCTOBER 11

From the oversize windows of the sunroom, Tegan Hartwood took one last look at the crashing waves below the bluffs, put down her moist watercolor brush, then excitedly descended to the second level of her beachfront house in Carlsbad and hurried to unlock the door to her special room.

Once inside, she opened the waiting designer shoebox, reassured that the dazzling, incandescent spike heels she had so carefully chosen for tonight would be the perfect finishing touch to her silver dress.

Her mouth automatically watered as lights from the huge crystal chandelier shined down on her brand new silver stunners, and the shoes responded by reflecting colors from the hundreds of other shoes in the vast collection that surrounded them. She could almost taste these new ones and felt the familiar reflexive thrill as she slid her feet smoothly inside. She swallowed and was satiated by their delectable glow. These shoes are gorgeous and so am I, she knew, as she gazed into the seven-foot free-standing mirror. The current culture, through movies, commercials and ads had conditioned men to respond to a certain look and she definitely had that look.

She swished her long, copper blonde hair from side to side, then admired the slender hips and solid, perky figure she worked so hard to maintain. She hadn't needed any cosmetic surgery so far, not even a breast lift. She flinched at the thought of her recent Botox and laugh line injections. It's taking a little more effort, time and money lately, she thought, but I still look twenty years younger than my calendar age.

These shoes make 461 pairs, she noted, gazing at the universe of intoxicating colors, bold patterns and rich textures captured in the shoes, many of which were true works of art. She looked slowly around the room at her collection of intricately detailed shoes that lined shelves on all four walls, evoking an air of indolent luxury.

There were shoes by Balenciaga, Zanotti, Prada, Blahnik, Choo, Fendi, Versace, Louboutin, Guinness, and Spade to name a few. Each pair connected her to the specific memory of a holiday, celebratory dinner, art gallery exhibit, one of her parties or, best of all, to a special man.

From ankle cuff sandals, triple buckle gladiators, asymmetrical slings, jeweled caged platforms, heels with studs and spikes, stacked wedges, peep toe platforms, wraparound ankle strap heels to fashion-forward ballet flats, the range of styles stunned visitors favored enough to be shown her prized collection, usually a client who had recently purchased one of her strikingly beautiful seascape paintings and who thus would appreciate these treasures as well.

For a few moments, her eyes rested on dramatic shoes of enviable height with crisscrossing turquoise satin straps embellished with tiny crystals. Next, a pair of fairy-tale-like shoes filled with lace and ruffles snagged her attention. And then, a pair of gold sequined pumps brought her back to Alexander's caresses.

But when she switched her gaze to Louboutin's signature red bottom heels, the ultimate iconic shoes, she lingered longer, allowing herself to flash back to an incredible night with a 29-year-old CEO. *Ahhh, Francesco!* That was during a vacation in Italy, when she had immersed herself in all things Italian, including the men, and had picked up the expression, "Arrivederci, mi amore," her favorite goodbye line whenever dumping a man.

She purred as she contemplated the adventure ahead, caressing her iridescent shoes after removing them. More than a date with a tall, broad-shouldered young man, their tryst tonight would be an event.

This particular catch had put up a nonchalant front for months at the Sea and Shore Fitness Center, where she worked part-time as a fitness trainer and Pilates instructor. He'd ignored her flirtatious ways and suggestive manner of speaking, and when she'd invited him to see her latest watercolor painting, he had flatly turned her down.

But things had a way of changing, didn't they?

She remembered that he had begun looking at her in a different way, as if seeing her for the first time, about three weeks ago. And then, one week ago, in what might seem like a sudden bazaar turnaround to almost any other woman, he took the lead and approached her as she was walking toward the women's locker room. He said he realized they were meant to get together and that he had some free time the following Friday. His move, of course, was no surprise to her; she knew he was already hers. He simply had needed a little time to figure that out.

Oh, how she relished carefully selecting the men in her life and the younger they were, the better. They'd always come back, begging to see her, and she'd let them, until they had fed her ego enough. Then her own attraction to them would fade and she'd callously dump them, no warning given, leaving a trail of bewildered men in her wake, most of them hoping to be taken back into her arms one day. She was most content with her carefree lifestyle. What could be better than plenty of money in the bank, and nothing and no one to tie her down—no husband, no kids, no pets, no live plants inside the house—precisely the way she'd always wanted it. One narrow escape had been more than enough. But she had taken care of that.

I moved here to live the lifestyle I want, she thought. No responsibilities, no strings, no worries.

Now, thanks to healthy eating, exercise, and great genes responsible for her killer looks, she didn't mind admitting she had turned 49, and watching the startled reactions.

Her three-story home in Southern California overlooked the beach, pompously staring down at the khaki sand below. She loved the top floor with its surrounding windows and panoramic ocean view, which she had turned into an art studio where she painted and invited serious prospective and current clients to view her work by appointment only.

In addition to the shoe collection room, the second level had a huge master bedroom, a comfortable guest room, two bathrooms and an exercise room complete with the latest machines and equipment.

A massive kitchen with a super-long L-shaped counter, tailor-made for the buffet-style parties she loved to throw, dominated the first level. There were also a great room, a formal dining room, a living room, and a powder room. The shapes, colors and textures throughout the house created an artistic picture. Natural stone floors were everywhere except in the lushly carpeted bedrooms and in the grand entrance area with its marbled flooring.

Outside on the sundeck, a round stone and metal table with a central fire pit provided seating for ten. On one side were a built-in barbecue area and a full bar.

So this would be the night. Fantasy would soon become reality. After a light lunch, Tegan slipped into her black spandex pants, pulled on a white top with the words Sea & Shore Fitness written across it in black, tied her fancy Nike sneakers, and walked back to the garage.

Ten minutes later, she parked her midnight blue Maserati and strutted into the gym, aware of the men's eyes, in plenty of time to teach one of her popular classes.

A woman was leaving the fitness center at the same time. Tegan automatically glanced down at her footwear.

Flip-flops! The original plain, rubber thong kind with no flair, no imagination, she thought.

Why, I wouldn't be caught dead in those shoes!

2

FIVE WEEKS EARLIER, SEPTEMBER 6

"*I*n nomine Patris, et Filie, et Spiritus Sancti, Amen. My son, what have you come to confess?"

"Forgive me, Father, for I have sinned; I was led into temptation and broke my vow of chastity."

"What was the occasion of your sin?"

"The woman came here to the rectory at night…"

"While I was away?"

"Yes. It was no secret around Saint Michael's that you were planning to attend a conference out of town."

"And you invited her to come in?"

"She had new clothing and toys in several boxes to donate for needy children in our parish. I was alone, tired and vulnerable. Once inside, she took advantage of that."

"Are you sorry for your grievous sin, for breaking your sacred commitment to God?"

"There is no worse sadness than knowing I have pierced our Lord's heart."

"What will you do if she wants to see you again?"

Silence.

"Do you promise to amend your life by never allowing such a union again?"

"It will never happen again."

"Good. Do you have any other past or current sins to confess?"

"I am troubled by lingering anger and my desire for retaliation for what she did to my life. She sullied my relationship with God."

"Don't harbor bitterness—it will eat away at you like poison and eventually paralyze you from moving forward. Forgive and let it go into God's hands."

"There must be payment for sin," Father Steven said. "This woman preys upon much younger men. Shouldn't such a person be prevented from continuing in her chosen lifestyle?"

"God is merciful, but He is also just. Let Him determine the consequences for her sins, not you. He has built into life a set of unchangeable natural laws that punish evildoers one way or another."

"Maybe justice will prevail sooner rather than later." Father Steven Caffrey could feel his stomach muscles tighten.

"God does not run on our schedule. Wait."

"Yes, Father, I see that now."

"You must disallow any thoughts of revenge from fermenting. After all, there's also a good chance that one day, for any number of reasons, she will be unable to continue such a lifestyle. Should that day come, she will be alone in a meaningless life. Perhaps then, in her ultimate feelings of despair, she will ask God for forgiveness, change her ways, and be saved."

Unless her heart already has been hardened to the point that it is impossible for her to turn around, Father Steven thought. In that case, she eventually may reach an age where she is no longer attractive to young men. What would she do then? Start paying? No thrill of conquest there!

"You must ask God now to forgive you for what you have done."

After saying the Act of Contrition, Father Steven was given absolution as well as a heavy penance. Then he left Father James Machiatelli's study quietly.

The older priest's forehead crinkled as he removed his stole. I wonder who this woman is. Could she be the one who stays in her pew during Communion and hungrily scrutinizes Steven as he walks back and forth distributing the sacred host to our parishioners while they're kneeling at the railing?

Back in his own room, Steven knelt down beside his bed. The guilt had been a stench in his nostrils, making him pay for his sin on the installment plan. Father Machiatelli was right. An evil act bears within itself its own punishment.

Why had he succumbed to Tegan Hartwood?

He resented the fact that all priests were put on the defensive because of the molestation stories. You felt as if you had to somehow make it clear you were not a pervert, he thought. You were a normal man, attracted to women, who had sacrificially and courageously decided to take the vow of chastity and become a Roman Catholic priest.

The Church has undergone more than enough disgrace because of the evil actions of some men who never should have become priests, he knew. What I've done can never be discovered and I've got to do my best to see to that. I cannot contribute to the Church's damaged reputation.

Now he prayed, "Lord God, forgive me. I've been on a detour but I want to get back on the right road. I've missed you."

As he rose, he added, "May you repay her for what she has done."

3

*T*he man stood stark still, staring, transfixed, at the collage of color photos that was on display, honoring the newly-chosen Instructor of the Year. If anyone else had been standing in the Sea & Shore Fitness Center's hallway at nine o'clock on the same Friday morning, the onlooker would have thought the man was about to have a stroke.

Initially, he'd only given them a cursory look. But now, one of them caught his eye; something about it made him stop and study the photo intently.

He looked a long time, feeling an uncomfortable stirring in the pit of his stomach. His eyes glazed over as if he were in a dazed space, a strange dimension, here but not really here. A realization was poised upon the rim of his conscious-ness but had not yet been able to slide through.

Then, like a flash of lightning across his brain cells, there was an instant of comprehension. In a profoundly sickening moment, a long-repressed truth rose up from the depths of his subconscious mind through the layers of more easily accessed memories and into his immediate consciousness. It was precisely then that he *knew.*

During these moments, the onlooker would have witnessed a radical change in the man's facial expression from curious to shocked to horrified. Contorted with rage, his normally attractive features twisted so that he appeared monstrous.

He blurted out something that fell like vanishing puffs into the unhearing air. But the empty hallway's gray walls absorbed his revelation—and so did his demons.

Ever since that moment of *knowing,* that split second in which soul and spirit were shattered, his mind had raced furiously ahead. The gnawing in his gut was like a rat gnawing at a rope. *Kill the rat, get on with your life.*

Over the course of the next several hours, he was able to put together an intricately ingenious plan. Justice would be satisfied *through him.*

To carry out all the steps necessary to achieve his goal, he calculated he would need three weeks. And by early that afternoon, he was already actively engaged in research on the internet.

Visualizing every move he would make opened a file in his brain, almost as if he'd already lived it. It would go even more perfectly during the real thing.

Instructor of the Year! She had been hitting on him for months now. Relentlessly. He always could see why all the other men at the gym watched every single move of her curvaceous body as she sauntered past the exercise machines after teaching one of her popular classes.

But rather than appealing to him, lately her aggression had triggered a reflexive repulsion, pushing some mysterious button even before seeing this photo. Gossip had long circulated at the gym that she was a cougar with the ability to reduce strapping, otherwise take-charge young men to putty before dropping them.

He'd been strong and kept his decision never again to allow his eyes to meet and linger with hers. That was before. Today, he reversed his decision.

4

*B*y now, fourteen days into his meticulous preparations, he finally set their date for the following Friday. This would give her a polite one week's notice while he would use these remaining seven days for last-minute details. When he told her he was looking forward to getting together, she responded with a triumphant, staccato laugh.

"Great! How about a dress-up dinner at eight—Sea Bass, black rice, steamed artichokes?"

"Sounds healthy. I'll bring the wine and my famous tabbouleh salad. It will complement the taste of the fish."

This step taken, he left the gym and drove to the beach.

During the past two weeks, he had poured every waking moment outside of doing his job into working out the minute details and logistics of his plan. His rage was not the kind that leads to an explosion and then it's over; it was a sustained emotional state that fed upon itself and provided the charge of almost supernatural energy he needed.

Now, as the man strode across the sand toward the double jetty on South Ponto Beach, he congratulated himself for sticking to his strict schedule in preparation for retribution day.

While Tegan was at work in the gym, he had timed the drive from the back of her house to this carefully chosen family beach in Carlsbad. He also had checked the road alongside the beach several times at precisely ten o'clock at night for traffic flow and possible police car activity. In the month of October, with few tourists and no holidays in sight, it was dead along this particular stretch of North Pacific Coast Highway 101.

He had noticed a *No Parking 11pm-5am* sign about 50 yards south in a pull-up area for people who wanted to enjoy the beach. He'd be long gone before eleven o'clock.

During the various times of day the man had practiced walking on top of the jetty toward the ocean, he couldn't help but notice names as well as hearts carved on the tops of many of the rocks. Etched into a few were short proclamations of loyalty and love. People love markers, he thought, something to show posterity that they were here, existed, mattered.

Now, starting from the first flat rock at the beginning of the jetty, he counted exactly 22 steps, with three to four steps per rock, to reach the precise, predetermined location where he would have to turn to the right. Then, he began to inch his way down the jetty's inner side that flanked the channel. Over his right shoulder was a weighted sack, filled with Idaho baking potatoes, which he held onto with his right hand to remind himself to concentrate on keeping his balance since he would only have one free hand.

Fishermen who effortlessly made their way down the side of the jetty in flip flops did not have to carry anyone over their shoulder. He had purchased special athletic sneakers made for basketball/volleyball players who needed full support for their fast side to side movements and awkward shifts of the feet.

It was getting dark. The rocks were angled in such a way that he could scoot from one rock down to the next and the next, like a child inching down a staircase one step at a time, until he reached the rock where he would lay her body.

This was his third practice run and he'd already memorized every move he would make. A full moon was predicted for next Friday but in the event the prediction was off, he was not about to take any chance of not finding his chosen rock in the unlit area.

A couple of feet above the current water level was the perfect spot: a fairly flat rock, approximately the length of her body, wedged between two protruding rocks. The rock that would be in back of her head jutted up about two feet higher than the flat rock. Another rock, juxtaposed at an angle like a footboard, would be underneath her feet, supporting her as she lay there. It rose one-and-a-half feet.

Tegan's final resting place had been tailor-made for her: An open-air casket which would ensure that her body could not accidentally slide into the channel between the two jetties and get swept off by the undertow, away from the ocean and toward the Batiquitos Lagoon.

Oh no, that would be too quick and easy, he thought. The horror of impending death must last long enough for her to silently confess her great sin—her mortal sin—and beg for forgiveness.

That's where the poison would come in.

Her eyes would look toward the two bridges under which the channel water ran toward the lagoon on the other side of the highway. This positioning was purposeful so that she would not be able to gauge which of the incoming ocean waves would randomly send a rush of water able to reach high enough to actually wash over her face.

The plan was to gently lay her there before ten-thirty, while the tide was still relatively low but well on its way back up. Then, and most importantly, he would abandon her to the whims of nature.

A most suitable mode of death!

He congratulated himself as he envisioned how the night would play out. The tide would slowly rise. Ocean waves would slap their way down the side of the jetty, a few of them intermittently reaching her level and washing over her. But she would never be totally submerged. No, there would be plenty of time in between the waves for sheer terror.

At one-thirty in the morning, the tide would reach its peak, then start slowly receding for the next five to six hours. By seven o'clock, it would be low. But since tomorrow would be a Saturday, probably her body wouldn't be noticed until much later, during high tide when local fishermen would set up their gear along the channel in hopes of catching halibut.

Climbing back up the side of the jetty to its top, he stood for several minutes surveying her rocky deathbed and reviewing his accomplishments so far. Seaweed and kelp danced wildly below the umber and gray rocks.

The jetty saw him and writhed.

As he walked back along the jetty, then across the sand toward his car, he envisioned how she would lie there, helpless, as the merciless tide swelled and splashed over her body. She would be in constant fear of the sporadic intervals during which the seawater would roll over her mouth. She would know that it would be impossible to hold her breath whenever that happened and then to exhale as the water subsided. Instead, in her paralyzed condition, she would have to allow the water free access.

Unless she dies from the poison before that happens, he thought. Death will be caused either by paralysis of her lungs or by drowning, whichever comes first.

He ruminated about how she would look. And as he heard himself laugh, he remembered back when he was growing up how other kids had made fun of his peculiar high frequency whiney sounds.

Fete accompli. Everything is already accomplished, the feat is done. I only need to walk forward into it.

His words were inscribed on the wind.

5

*T*he man's research on poisons had been fruitful. For his specific purpose, Spotted Hemlock was ideal. An interesting plant, beautiful on the outside with its white flowers, but evil on the inside—exactly like her, he thought. It is common along roadsides on the Pacific Coast.

Known also as Poison Hemlock, Devil's Bread, and Poison Parsley, hemlock's leaves look as innocent as parsley. Hemlock contains coniine, which accounts for much of its acute toxicity. Within thirty to forty minutes of ingestion, a victim's central nervous system is disrupted. The legs feel heavy first. Then the poison creeps upward, weakening and paralyzing muscles as it ascends, until it eventually reaches the lungs, cutting off oxygen to the heart and brain.

But it does not kill for up to several hours after intake. Sometimes it causes blindness, but whether it would or not was of no importance. The real cornerstone to his plan was that she would remain fully conscious, utterly tormented until the end.

On this Thursday morning, he picked the hemlock and then shopped for the additional ingredients for the tabbouleh salad. Everything had to be fresh so it would look and smell delicious. He positioned his mask, then slipped on gloves for protection against possible absorption of toxins by his skin and lungs.

Of the several recipes he'd selected and tried, this one was by far the most tantalizing. She would love it.

TABBOULEH

Wash parsley, dry with paper towels, remove stems.
Finely chop Persian cucumbers, tomatoes, red onion, and garlic.
Add quinoa, lemon vinaigrette, salt and pepper.
Mix all ingredients together. Let flavors meld overnight in fridge.

But all these preparations, in addition to the regular work he always had to do, had made the days longer and harder. When he finally hit the sheets at night, he immediately dozed off.

But then, there were the nightmares.

6

*T*he man arrived precisely at eight o'clock. When Tegan Hartwood opened the door, he took in all five foot seven of her with one sweeping glance: the coppery hair, cobalt eyes, plunging neckline, and long slender legs. She couldn't weigh more than 120 pounds. Perfect.

"This will be a night to remember," she purred, accepting his bottle of Chardonnay and covered dish with the tabbouleh, and then starting toward the dining room.

Yes, he thought, a night you'll get the shock of your life, you evil, soulless bitch. You cannot continue to destroy one more person's spirit.

"Everything's almost ready. Will you pour the wine?" she asked, heading toward the kitchen.

While waiting, he forked the right amount of tabbouleh onto her salad plate and then took a lesser amount from the container for his own salad plate. He would, after all, not be consuming any.

Tonight there are a full moon and a favorable movement of high and low tides, he knew. This late dinner fits neatly into all my scheduled plans. It will be close to nine when we consume our desserts. That's when she thinks I will become easy prey in a wild sex binge but that connection is not going to happen. I'll play along and then, after dinner, while relaxing on the sofa, I'll announce my big surprise.

As she returned, carrying their two steaming hot dinner plates, he smiled broadly.

This will be your last night on earth and the beginning of your eternal hell.

7

*H*er slight stagger as she approached him was the first sign that the coniine was kicking in. He had purposely lingered over the tiramisu so that now it was thirty-two minutes since her last mouthful of salad. He allowed her to slowly begin to unbutton his shirt, knowing that's as far as she would get.

"I must have overdone it today. My knees feel as if they're buckling," she said thickly.

He felt her pulse. It was rapid and weak.

"Let's sit down," said the man, taking her by the arm and leading her to the sofa in the living room. "It's time to talk."

He poured out his memorized script with a rhythm that kept perfect pace with the physical stiffening of her limbs. He watched malevolently as she tried to interrupt his torrent of angry words but was unable to summon the energy.

By the time he finished speaking, her body was slumped helplessly on the sofa cushion. Muscular paralysis had set in but her mind was alert and cognition would remain intact until the end.

She opened her mouth as if ready to scream. Silence. Her features contorted, eyes widened, and eyebrows arched in shock. Reminds me of one of the world's most famous paintings, *The Scream*, by Edvard Munch, he mused.

Laying her down on the couch, he slipped on the disposable latex gloves in the inside pocket of his jacket, then went into the kitchen to hand-wash and dry their dishes and glasses and place them back into their accustomed spots in the kitchen cabinets.

Investigating eyes would not have a clue about who had been there that night. He washed and dried the empty bottle of Chardonnay. Earlier, he had been scrupulous about not touching the dining table or anything else that could reveal prints. With a couple of paper towels, he quickly polished the few surfaces he'd touched.

Now he walked out to the garage where his rental car was waiting and opened the back seat door. How foolish of her to have let him park there while she was busy in the kitchen! Quickly walking back inside with his gloves still on, he carried her out to the car and carefully placed her on top of the opened blanket that lay across the back seat. Her body was rigid and cold.

He looked into her staring eyes.

"I'm taking you to your grave. I will abandon you there. By the time they discover you tomorrow, you will look like a puffer fish."

8

*P*eggy Conti Crawford stood on the moist hard sand, looking down at the base of the southernmost of the twin jetties that beautifully decorated South Ponto Beach. She was captivated by the clusters of tiny black clams, mussels piggybacking their baby mussels, and lichened rocks that were only revealed during low tide.

She couldn't wait to see Barb and Cassie and had arrived a few minutes before seven o'clock. Each of the three best friends had a fully booked day ahead so they'd decided on an early morning get-together.

The plaintive cries of a seagull caught her attention and she turned toward the sea to watch as the bird veered sharply over the swell of the surf to snatch a morsel floating with the breeze. This time of day, the air was still cool and crisp and the ocean's navy blue depth lines sharply contrasted with cerulean tones. The horizon line was indistinguishable and shrouded in mist.

Peggy pulled the zipper on her lightweight jacket all the way up and breathed in the salty air. The attractive, petite blonde, who worked part time as a reference librarian, was upbeat by nature and had a strong sense of adventure. There was so much to catch up on. Time had swallowed and digested a couple of months since all three baby boomers had been able to get together for their usual twice-monthly *walk and talks* along the various SoCal beaches. During those walks over the past several years, they probably had discussed every possible topic related to life after fifty with all of its changes and challenges, as well as the situations in their own everyday lives. And they'd done so with encouragement, understanding and generous helpings of laughter.

No rocking chairs yet, she smiled to herself, not for us. We're not about to let age become a reference point against which we measure how we feel, look, what we want to achieve, what we are capable of doing and dreaming.

Cassie's wedding had been followed by an extended honeymoon with Nicholas Korba in Texas. Soon afterward, fresh from her course in conversational Italian, Barb had taken off to Italy for 24 days with her two teenage granddaughters. Later, Peggy was the one missing from the threesome when she flew to Carmel, Indiana to be with her mother.

As soon as they arrived, there were big hugs and some quick small talk.

"Let's go out to the tip of the jetty first," suggested Cassie, "so I can take some pics of you two with the panoramic ocean view as a backdrop. With no definitive horizon line, the blues and greens seem to melt into the sky like an impressionistic painting."

Barb chuckled. "Cassie, don't you have more than enough photos bursting out of albums without adding more? I mean with your wedding and honeymoon shots and all?"

Peggy led the way, quickly climbing the gray, ochre, and burnt umber rocks to the top of the jetty. As she stepped from rock to rock, she carefully avoided the deep openings in between some of them, which unfortunately housed soda cans, potato chip bags and candy wrappers that had not yet been removed by State maintenance crews.

About halfway along, she side-stepped over to a rock on the far right side of the jetty. "Mack caught two halibuts right down there," she announced, pointing downward. "He said during high tide the current in the channel between these jetties is so strong the fish float straight to the fishermen's baits."

As she pointed downward, Peggy's attention was suddenly riveted in one spot. "Oh, my dear God!" she shouted as she started inching her way down the rocks for a closer look.

"What? What is it?" Cassie and Barb almost responded in unison as they peered over the edge of the jetty and watched their friend descend.

The body of a woman lying flat in a cradle of rocks was unmistakable. It almost seemed that her skin was metallic so tightly did her soaking wet silver dress cling to every bone and curve. Her long copper blonde hair was splayed out in strands. Mascara was puddled like black watercolor underneath her eyes. Her arms were flailed outward, her legs were metal-rod straight.

"I don't think she's alive," Peggy called out. "She looks dead!"

Barb started down the rocks. As soon as she saw the bloated, wrinkled face, limp limbs, closed eyes, and slack jaw, she realized the answer to Peggy's question without having to first check for a heartbeat.

"This is horrible. It's too late for resuscitation," she knew, having seen more than enough dead patients before recently retiring from her long career as a nurse practitioner. She also did not have a shred of doubt that the woman had been dead for some time.

"What an awful accident; she must have slipped," said Cassie, gazing down from her perch on an angled rock at the top of the jetty and pulling her cell phone from her waistband. "I'll call for an ambulance to transport her body to the morgue."

As Cassie stepped to a flatter rock in the center of the jetty, something shiny, adjacent to one of the nearby crevices caught her attention. Bending down, she was dazzled by a shoe that had narrowly escaped falling into the crack and had landed at an angle which allowed the sunlight to play across its metallic leather surface and create a shimmering spectrum of colors. The sole of the shoe was practically pristine.

This is the most stunning, iridescent shoe I've ever seen, she thought. But what woman in her right mind would ever attempt to wear spike heels on a jetty? What's it doing here and where's the other shoe?

"What do you make of this?" she called down to her friends as she held the shoe up high by its skinny long heel. "I don't see the other shoe anywhere."

Peggy stared at the shoe, then back at Cassie, with an expression of horror.

"The other shoe is not missing; it's on this woman's foot. Don't call for an ambulance, call the police.

"This was no accident. This was murder!"

As she waited for the police to arrive, Cassie put the shoe back down, then quickly shot pictures of the crime scene from various angles, zooming in to include the victim's full body as well as close-ups of her face, framed by a limp, tangled mass of hair.

No sooner did she finish than two police squad cars pulled up. Sliding her iPhone into one of the zippered pockets of her cargo pants, Cassie followed Peggy and Barb, who were already down on the sand walking toward the officers.

9

By the time 34-year-old Carlsbad Police Sergeant Blane Sandingis strode across the jetty some twenty minutes later, both the sandy side and the street side of the south jetty were cordoned off. Photos and video had been shot, the crime scene measured, and the women's statements recorded by two of his investigators from the Crimes of Violence Unit. The medical examiner was on his way.

After immediately studying the crime scene and reviewing notes taken, the lead homicide detective ordered the north jetty to also be cordoned off. This would prevent anyone with a camera or iPhone from climbing it for a view of the body from the other side of the channel.

He had his own questions for the women, who had been directed to wait behind the draped yellow tape.

"So you say the three of you were out here at seven to take some pictures when you discovered the body. Did any of you touch that shoe?" He pointed to the top of the jetty.

"I barely picked it up for a minute to show Peggy and Barb, then put it right back," Cassie answered defensively.

"Back *precisely* where you found it? How sure are you?" The detective was clearly miffed.

"It's seared in my mind."

This time Sandingis looked directly at Peggy. "The first officers to arrive tell me you're convinced this woman was murdered. What makes you so certain?"

"It's the only scenario that makes any sense."

"How so?"

"First of all, even if she was foolish enough to attempt to walk across the top of this jetty at night in five-inch heels—extremely unlikely—how and why would she have hobbled down the side with only one shoe on?"

"Go on."

"Secondly, why would she choose to lie there all night long and allow herself to die?"

"Maybe she was drunk."

"With no apparent scrapes or cuts to indicate she had stumbled? And another thing, if that were the case, how would she have been able to select and then neatly position herself between these two particular rocks so she would not fall into the sea? She just lay there, let her lungs fill up? Come on, Detective, who would do that?"

Sandingis locked his hands behind his head. "Since you're playing detective, did you consider suicide?"

"Oh, sure," Peggy shot back. "She got all dressed up to the nines, walked across all these rocks and crevices in spikes in the dark, lost one shoe, and then hobbled down the side of the jetty in her remaining shoe until she reached that specific rock where she could lie down until she died."

While they talked, the medical examiner, along with his crime lab tech, pulled up close to the jetty. Behind his vehicle, an ambulance with two EMS team members arrived to take the body to the morgue as soon as it was officially released.

Sandingis looked at Peggy and her friends with mounting interest. "Wait here. I'll get back to you after I finish with the ME."

"Oh, by the way, Detective Sandingis," Peggy couldn't stop herself from adding, "if she drove herself here, where is her car? The nearest parked cars are about 150 feet from the jetty. Right now, I only see five cars. Three of them are ours and I'll bet the other two belong to a couple of persons out for an early walk."

This Peggy Crawford is somewhat sassy but very sharp, Sandingis thought, as he turned around and started back up the jetty. It's only natural she is already mentally and emotionally involved in this case after her intense shock. But I hope she doesn't get in my way or worse, put herself and her friends in danger.

10

*L*ing Chen had scarcely gotten back from walking Delphinium, her Italian Blue Greyhound, at eight-fifteen Saturday morning when the phone rang.

"Ling, this is Mark Evanston at *Seaside Magazine*. We've gotten a tip from a reliable source out at South Ponto Beach about a probable murder on one of the two jetties there. If you want first crack at the story while initial impressions are sharp and people are more apt to talk, it's yours."

"I'm on my way, as soon as I put down some food and fresh water for Delph. I can get there in about fifteen minutes."

"Well, hurry up," said the editor in his usual brusque tone. "Once word gets out, Ponto Beach will be swarmed with media. They'll get the basic news but they won't get all of the juicy minutiae you can unearth.

"Look, I need a quick reaction piece to run in our online edition today. Then you can update it for our print magazine right before we go to press Wednesday."

"Got it."

"Much more important, how would you feel about writing an investigative feature story about the murder, along with plenty of in-depth interviews—your specialty? You'd have as much space as you need."

Ling's heart was pounding. "What's my deadline?"

"I want the big story to be ready to go as soon as an arrest is made. So you have until then."

After running a brush through her pitch black reverse bob, Ling swished some blush over her cheeks and applied lip gloss. She was certainly a minimalist when it came to makeup, she realized, as she looked in the powder room mirror

26

at her classic Taiwanese almond-shaped chocolate brown eyes, bare of any liner or eye shadow. *No man is going to experience a lightning bolt moment with me.*

"See you later, Delph," she said, grabbing her sunglasses, sunhat and purse. She patted her sweet companion affectionately and rushed out the door of her townhouse.

Before moving to North County San Diego seven months ago, 29-year-old Ling had worked as a freelance feature story writer in Pittsburgh, where she was known in print media circles for her deep-digging investigative abilities. Editors from a variety of magazines as well as newspapers kept the assignments coming. They also appreciated that she would come up with many of her own story ideas. She was a skilled interviewer able to perceive a slant for a story no one else saw.

But then, after a protracted and nasty divorce, the Taiwanese woman wanted to get as far away as possible from the city of inclines and start fresh somewhere completely different. One year after the divorce, she did exactly that.

Career-wise, she had known what that would mean. For writers, it's always back to square one when you move. No matter how good you were someplace else, you must prove yourself all over again.

I've done some fairly interesting stories here in SoCal so far for some good media outlets, but nothing with the potential that this story has, she realized. *This is my big chance to get back to my peak level and it's also North County Seaside Magazine's opportunity to shine!*

By eight thirty-five when Ling drove up, flashing lights and police activity at the south jetty had attracted curious onlookers, comprised of some who happened to be driving by and others arriving for a day at the beach.

Confidently approaching the nearest officer, Ling introduced herself and asked if she could speak with the detective in charge.

"You'll have to wait, ma'am. He's at the bottom of the other side of this jetty with the ME. Could be a long while."

"Can you please point out the person who discovered the body? I assume he or she is still here."

"Actually, those three ladies talking over there are the ones who called it in," he said, pointing them out in the growing crowd.

"Thank you, officer."

11

"Well, Mike, what do you think so far?" Sandingis leaned forward from an adjacent rock, his eyes surveying the body.

The ME, Dr. Mike Attison, was conducting his examination, "At this point, I'd estimate her death as between midnight and one this morning. Keep in mind that the tide reached its highest peak at one-thirty."

"Any theories?"

"She must have been carried down here wrapped in a protective covering of some sort, probably between ten and ten-thirty last night, while that higher rock she's lying on was still only slightly moist."

"Why so?"

"She is in almost pristine condition, except for the obvious effects of over-exposure to water on her face and body. Eyes closed, flat on her back, no wounds, scrapes, bruises, or contusions. Even more interesting, not one rip or snag in her clothing."

Sandingis' eyes focused on the white froth at her mouth and nose. "What about the cause of death? Drowning?" He paused. "Drugs? Anything apparent?"

"There are absolutely no signs of struggle."

"So she could have been rendered helpless before being placed down here," Sandingis said, closely following the ME's deductive reasoning.

"And in that case, any inrush of water into her larynx could have caused a laryngeal spasm. She wouldn't have been able to get any oxygen.

"On the other hand, she could have been DOA."

"You're leaning toward…?"

"We'll see back in the lab.

"I need to get her out of here ASAP, while the tide is still low enough, so my tech can thoroughly examine the rock she is lying on as well as the rocks starting from here on up to the spot where her other shoe dropped. Although, in this setting, it's pretty doubtful we will find trace evidence like blood from a scratch. If there was a killer, he probably wore gloves."

"Make this case a priority, Mike. Forget about this weekend with the family. I'm putting a rush on finding out what went down here."

"Right. An immediate autopsy with a drug screen."

12

"If only you could have seen her," Peggy blurted out after Ling walked over, introduced herself, and explained her story assignment.

"She was lying on a rock...lots of algae tangled in her long copper hair, sopping-wet silver dress that looked like liquid steel, and wearing only the one shoe with its five-inch heel. I knew she was dead the minute I saw her."

"The first thing I thought after the initial shock—limp limbs, thin foam around her open mouth, no pulse..." added Barb, "this type of crime suggests a simmering hatred that reached its boiling point where the killer went over the edge and staged such a painstakingly elaborate scene."

"His?"

Barb answered confidently. "Unless a six-foot-eight lesbian dragged her down here, my guess is it would take a strong man to carry her across the jetty and down the rocks, then lay her down so gently there wasn't a mark on her. Maybe the guy she dressed up for."

"Right," said Peggy, "she wasn't wearing a wedding band or engagement ring."

Ling's investigative antennae were fully engaged. "The three of you seem to believe without a doubt she was murdered."

"Looking at this logically," said Peggy, repeating for Ling what she'd told Sandingis.

"You mentioned she had only one shoe on?"

"I found the other one," chimed in Cassie.

"Where was it?"

"Perched on the edge of one of the rocks at the top of the jetty."

"Ahhh, and that's why you think she was being carried. One shoe accidentally dropped off," considered Ling.

"Which leads me to wonder whether she was already dead or at least unconscious or drugged when she was laid on that rock," added Peggy.

The *Seaside Magazine* editor had been right. Getting there before the rest of the media was giving Ling a running start in laying the foundation for her story. Peggy and her two friends had provided descriptive information of the corpse, exactly how she looked while lying there, which she would not have been privy to otherwise, since no one was being allowed beyond the yellow tape. They even had pictures of the overall crime scene as well as of the shoe.

Ling sensed that these three women would continue to be allies as she constructed her in-depth feature story layer by layer to its final conclusion over the next days, maybe weeks.

Some commotion on top of the jetty caught Ling's attention as two men carried a stretcher with the covered body from the jetty to the ambulance. Now was her opportunity to speak with the lead detective on the case. Luckily, he was headed toward them now.

13

"Ms. Crawford, I wanted you to wait until the body was released so I could have a few words with you," Sandingis said in a deadly serious tone.

"The media will want to hear about your discovery. If you and your friends release your names, expect them to be made public. For your own safety, it will be better if you do not provide names or any other personal information."

I don't want them exposing themselves to any possible danger unnecessarily, Sandingis thought. The criminal mind is unpredictable.

A large TV news network truck drove up and screeched to a stop, diverting Sandingis' attention. The few original onlookers had grown to a crowd of dozens.

"As soon as the rest of the press arrives and sets up, I'll be making a statement that should take care of most of your questions. You're welcome to stick around," he told Peggy, getting ready to walk away.

Ling, who had backed up so the detective could speak directly to Peggy, found herself looking at Sandingis' back. But she knew she would have to ask her top question fast. All the rest of the vultures would be arriving any second.

"Was drowning the cause of death or could it have been something else?" she called out.

Sandingis wheeled around to respond.

"You are?"

"Ling Chen for *North County Seaside Magazine*."

"Good question. I've ordered both toxicology and pathology examinations."

"So you have some indication that the victim may have been drugged?"

Ling's follow-up question hung in the air as the TV reporter and cameraman first to arrive now aggressively positioned themselves directly in front of Sandingis.

"Detective Sandingis, was this a murder?" the reporter asked.

"This certainly is a suspicious death but we can't officially state murder or anything definitive until the autopsy is complete. Now if you'll be patient, I have a few more things to do before the rest of the media arrive."

Looking back at Ling, Sandingis mouthed the word *sorry*, gave a slight nod and then turned away, ducked under the tape, and climbed back up the jetty. Ling watched as he stooped to pick something up. From way down on the sand where they were standing, there was no way that pushy TV reporter could have guessed what it was or how important it might become to the case. Thanks to Peggy's heads-up, Ling had the advantage.

Holding the shoe, Sandingis walked to the opposite edge of the jetty, where he stood stark still, staring down at the now empty crime scene.

14

Within the next ten minutes, the beach was peppered with crews from TV stations as well as with print media reporters.

"Do you know who the deceased woman is?"

"Was it death by drowning?"

"Who found the body?"

"What time did she die?"

"How old does she appear to be?"

"Was this a homicide?"

The questions were fast and furious.

Sandingis held his right hand up over his five-foot-eleven-inch medium-large frame. "As soon as the ME's report is ready, my office will contact the media with a statement. Meanwhile, I can assure you that this will be investigated as a suspicious death and every effort will be made to establish the identity of the deceased quickly. If anyone has information that could prove to be helpful, he or she should notify the Carlsbad police. What I can give you now is a detailed description of the dead woman.

"Who discovered the body?" shouted a young man with a camera.

"For their own protection, and so they won't be hounded by all of you, that person's name will not be released at this time."

"We'll find out eventually."

"Eventually, not now."

As Sandingis spoke, a TV reporter skirted around the throng until she reached Peggy, Barb, and Cassie. In a voice low enough not to be overheard by any of her competitors, she said, "I understand that you were the ones who found the body this morning…"

15

By six o'clock that Saturday night, the story was all over the news. Milburn Malawsky slumped into his recliner and stared at the TV news commentator. He'd had an especially grueling day as general manager of the Sea and Shore Fitness Center and wished he could simply call it a day.

"The body of an unidentified woman was discovered on one of the twin jetties at South Ponto Beach in Carlsbad at seven o'clock this morning by three women out for an early walk.

"The victim was described by police as Caucasian, five-feet-seven, athletically built, having long copper blonde hair, wearing a silver dress. Her shoes were metallic spike heels.

"There were no marks of violence on the body.

"Police are investigating the death as suspicious. An autopsy was ordered and the ME's report will be released as soon as available. Anyone who can help identify the victim or provide any information, no matter how insignificant you think it may be, is asked to immediately contact the Carlsbad police."

Milburn switched from one channel to another. The four major networks were all carrying the story as part of their local reports with slight variations, each of them including footage of Sandingis addressing the media and ending with panoramic views of the double jetty and ocean.

"Three friends taking pictures at South Ponto Beach early this morning were shocked to discover the body of a woman on the rocks of one of the two jetties on this friendly family beach."

"Oh no, that sounds like Tegan," Milburn shouted as he bounded out of his chair.

"Why Tegan? A lot of women living along the coast can be described in a similar way," said his wife.

The precise description of Tegan gave him no other choice than to call the police and identify her as his employee at the gym. If he didn't, he could easily become a person of interest. But first, he would try to reach her.

As Tegan's phone rang and rang, Milburn took comfort in knowing there would be a record of his attempt to reach her. And besides, Gloria would be a witness to the fact that he acted shocked to hear the bad news. All of which would demonstrate that he was a concerned, responsible employer.

Good thing Gloria had flown back home a couple of nights ago after a super long stay with her mother in Georgia. The trip had been necessitated by the fact that her mother lived alone and needed help following emergency gall bladder surgery. Not that he had minded Gloria's absence. It had been a welcome break not to have to hear his wife's alarm clock go off at four forty-five every morning. What an early bird he had married!

While he waited to be connected to the homicide unit, a feeling of peace coursed through his body. The constant threat that his one slip with Tegan could leak back to Gloria at any time had been a black cloud hanging over him day and night. That information had the potential to destroy his marriage. He had decided not to let himself be entrapped again. One thing Gloria would never tolerate was cheating.

Tegan had been so brazen afterward, continuing to prance around the gym like she owned the place, flirting with all the young, buff men, including him, knowing he certainly couldn't justify firing such a popular instructor to the owner of Sea and Shore Fitness without raising eyebrows.

First, there was her demand for a raise, later on for that huge color photo collage she audaciously hung up in the hallway to honor herself as Instructor of the Year. What on earth would have been next?

At 29, I didn't realize how inexperienced I was compared to that cougar's wildly imaginative moves, he thought. What a fool he was to have let himself be used for her subsequent blackmail. And whatever he learned about sex that fateful night months ago wasn't worth the risk of losing his wife.

He picked up his phone to access the Twitterverse.

I wonder how many of my instructors know. I've caught Becky smirking at me a few times since that night in my office, he recalled.

Now Tegan will not be bragging to anyone about this or any of her other conquests.

16

"The guy wore gloves while he washed and dried all the dishes and utensils and put them away neatly. Even this Chardonnay bottle in the trash can is wiped clean," summed up Officer George Wilkens as he searched Tegan Hartwood's kitchen cabinets in Sunday's early morning sunlight streaming in from the oversize windows.

"Sarge, everything matches except this one salad bowl."

Sandingis, who was peering inside the fridge, turned to take the bowl from Wilkens, at the same moment Officer Juan Dominguez finished dusting for prints in the great room, dining room, living room, and guest bathroom on the same floor.

"Find any, Dominguez?"

"No such luck, Sergeant. Totally the way you figured. We're dealing with a perfectionist."

Sandingis returned his full attention to the object in his right hand. "The probability of Tegan having purchased this bowl is practically zero. All her household décor and kitchenware are thoughtfully artistic—there's not one thing that isn't—except this."

"It's solid white, no style, plain as plain can be," Wilkens noted. "The kind of bowl anyone could have picked up at Target or Walmart."

"That was the idea."

As was his habit, the detective verbalized his train of thought out loud so his two homicide team detectives could follow along. "If this bowl belongs to the killer, I have to wonder if whatever was in it contained some sort of poison.

The perp had to keep his hands free to carry the victim. He had no other choice but to leave the bowl and wine bottle behind."

Sandingis sucked in his breath. "Look, a report from the ME as to whether or not Tegan was drugged or poisoned is imminent. If that turns out to be the case, even the smallest remaining speck of a matching substance would provide us hard evidence that the crime was initiated here by someone she dressed up for and invited for a dinner date."

"Someone she believed was equally attracted to her," said Wilkens.

"Someone who was some great actor," Dominguez added.

Sandingis walked over to the sink, pushed up his shirt sleeves, swabbed the inside of the garbage disposal, then gave the resulting sample to Wilkens to rush to Dr. Mike Attison at the crime lab for analysis.

Sandingis addressed both officers. "First thing tomorrow, I want you at the Sea and Shore Fitness Center. Find out about any of the victim's past or present hookups. Talk to the manager, receptionist, and other employees. While you two are busy doing that, I will be speaking to the members who were taking Tegan's classes."

By two o'clock, Sandingis was pacing the office floor when his iPhone rang. The ME's exuberant voice was exactly what he'd been waiting to hear.

"Our gut feeling was right," he boomed. "The victim's system was full of Poison Hemlock, and your speck from the garbage disposal is a match.

"No evidence of hanky-panky. Easy to surmise that the killer gave her the poison and then drove her directly to the beach."

"Any clues at all left on the jetty?"

"We finally found one navy blue wool thread after meticulously searching the victim's rocky deathbed. It must have caught as the killer was slowly rolling her out of the blanket. Unless the perp kept the blanket and you end up searching his domicile after narrowing down your suspect list to one guy, the thread won't help. Sorry."

As soon as he thanked Dr. Mike Attison, Sandingis sat down to prepare a statement for the press.

17

"How'd it go at the library this afternoon, babe?" Mack called out from the kitchen as he heard Peggy entering their home from the garage door.

"You mean except for the fact that I couldn't concentrate on my job?"

"Discovering a dead person on the beach yesterday was a shocking experience."

"I'm afraid that image will be popping into my head for a long time," said Peggy as she headed into the living room and grabbed the remote. "It's time for the evening news reports. Let's see if there's anything new."

"…and the woman has been identified as Tegan Hartwood, a Pilates instructor at Sea and Shore Fitness Center in Carlsbad and also a well-known artist throughout North County.

"Milburn Malawsky, manager of the center, confirmed her identity, stating that he was stunned and greatly saddened upon hearing of her death. He said photos were sent to the media a few weeks ago when she was alive and well and was named their Instructor of the Year."

Next, a video was played of Sandingis' press conference.

"The death of Tegan Hartwood, a 49-year-old Southern California artist and fitness instructor is being investigated as a murder. According to the ME"s report, released one hour ago, death was caused by respiratory failure. This could have been due to drowning or to the Poison Hemlock found in her system, whichever prevented her from breathing first.

"We have evidence that Ms. Hartwood ingested the poison in her own home and subsequently was taken by the perpetrator to one of the twin jetties on South Ponto Beach in Carlsbad on Friday night, October 11.

"North County residents can be assured that whoever committed this crime will be caught."

The newscaster summed up. *"Things like this don't happen on SoCal's friendly beaches and that's why this story is already attracting national attention."*

Peggy switched to another channel.

"Murder at the beach. Double jetty, double method," spouted the inexperienced young reporter, as clips of the two beautiful jetties rolled.

Without saying anything, Peggy started toward the study where she kept a large basket for their non-urgent mail and sorted through the growing pile excitedly. "Absolutely what I need," she shouted loud enough for Mack to hear from the other room.

In her hand was a large, glossy postcard from Sea and Shore Fitness. Splashed across the front was the promo: *Two Weeks Free Trial Membership for You and a Guest.*

Quickly texting her two friends, Peggy hoped at least one of them would be available on Wednesday, her free day this week. As a part-time reference librarian, she either worked mornings or afternoons—some of which extended into evening— six days a week. Her day off varied according to work load.

One answer arrived within minutes. This Wednesday, Cassie had a morning dental appointment and an afternoon tutoring session with one of her regular high school seniors.

Cassie loved her one-on-one time with students who paid attention and really wanted to learn. She focused on grammar and vocabulary building, believing if kids knew how to express their deepest emotions in words, there would be less misunderstanding and more harmony in their lives.

After years of teaching English in jam-packed classrooms where the behavior of the kids who had no intention whatsoever to learn anything distracted the others and devoured valuable class time, she knew she had made a wise career adjustment in time for the fall semester last year.

As Peggy waited anxiously to hear back from Barb, she wondered who had abandoned Tegan Hartwood to a certain death, either from poison or by drowning as tidal waves smacked into the jetty. And for what conceivable motive?

After eating the delicious dinner Mack had prepared, Peggy showered, laid out an outfit for her library shift the next morning, then joined him in the living room and relaxed with a light romantic comedy on a DVD he had ready for them to watch together. Mack always knows exactly what I need, she thought, cuddling next to him on the sofa.

As the DVD ended, she heard the welcoming sound of Barb's arriving text. Yes, she was available and couldn't wait to get started on Peggy's hunch that some answers were to be found at the gym.

"From what I recall about Poison Hemlock," Barb texted, *"this news means Tegan was brought to the jetty already paralyzed."*

That night in bed, Peggy tossed and turned for hours, glad Mack was a sound sleeper. This community of congenial neighbors and merchants deserve to have their sense of peace and security restored as quickly as possible, she believed. There must be something else I can do to help before Wednesday at the gym.

By tomorrow morning, she would know exactly what that was.

18

As if it were not enough to have to deal with his continuing feelings of guilt about having been snared by Tegan Hartwood, now Father Steven Caffrey had to hear her name all over the news.

He couldn't count the times he'd replayed the moment in time he broke his sacred vow. It was now more than five weeks ago that she had shown up at the rectory door with all those donations. Flashing back to the scene, he involuntarily shuddered. To him, it was happening again in real time. He could feel her cobalt eyes again, searing through his flesh as she removed her jacket and then pressed up against him. When he broke out in a sweat, she assured him all he was doing was expressing appreciation for her most charitable contribution to a worthy cause.

Two days later, during a private face-to-face confession, he had spilled his guts to Father James Machiatelli, crying like a little boy and promising never again to break his vow of chastity. That was one future sin the devil himself couldn't entice him to commit.

But afterward, why had she continued to approach him, once even in the courtyard where they served coffee and pastries after Mass? Was she thrilled by tormenting a Roman Catholic priest? Whatever her game, it was over and done with forever. The answers to those questions didn't matter anymore. All he wanted now was to be able to concentrate on his mission as a priest.

19

By early Monday morning, media coverage was in high gear. Competition was fierce. Ling knew it was time to start doing some undercover work with Peggy.

Her first story for *Seaside Magazine* had stirred a buzz with its revelation of intimate details about the victim and crime scene that none of the other reporters had been able to pick up. How did she know so much about Tegan Hartwood's dress, shoes, lack of a wedding ring, and positioning on the rocks?

But, true to her word, one bit of information Ling did not print was Peggy's identity. And she was grateful that Peggy had jotted down her name and work phone number before she and her friends slipped away from the TV crews two days ago at the jetty.

At nine-twenty, Peggy picked up the phone at the library reference desk on its first ring and immediately recognized Ling's slight Taiwanese accent.

"Peggy, I forgot to ask you if you happened to notice the designer's name inside that dropped shoe."

"Sure, Cassie said it was Marina Marison."

"Mmm. Never heard of that one."

"Neither had I. When I Googled it, I found out the designer is an emerging talent in the high-end women's shoe business. She launched with a huge splash and was picked up by guess who? Neiman Marcus. In fact, they're the only ones carrying this line so far. According to Cassie, Tegan's shoe on top of the jetty was definitely new. She must have bought them there."

"Wow, Peggy! You're doing half my job for me. Since we seem to be thinking along the same lines, let's find out which salesperson sold her those shoes and whether Tegan happened to have said anything noteworthy. Why don't I find out who it was and then we can go to the department store together during his or her work hours. I really want to do this interview before anyone else thinks of it."

"Great! I love trying on shoes."

Less than an hour later, Ling called back. "How would tomorrow early afternoon work for you?"

"I'll be finished here by one."

"I can pick you up from the library and we can head straight down there and ask Elisa Beckham to show us some of their most glamorous shoes. Turns out she's the saleslady who has been assisting Tegan with her choices for years."

As Ling clicked off, she thought about her work load over the next few weeks. Besides this major story, I've got to produce several other pieces already promised. Good thing those topics will be less demanding because the bulk of my energy and effort must go into this murder case.

The press is in a frenzy—like bloodhounds following the scent of a rabbit. What they don't know is I've arranged to meet with the woman who first saw the body on the jetty tomorrow, immediately after her early shift at the library.

20

*I*t was Monday afternoon when Roger Moore sat at a back table in Starbucks with a tall hazelnut Massiato and the newspaper. On the front page of an inside section was a large photo of the double jetty on Ponto Beach. His posture stiffened as the headline jumped out at him.

MURDER, THEY SAID

Three SoCal women discovered the dead body of a woman last Saturday morning at Ponto Beach. They were taking pictures from the top of the south jetty when they spotted the body near the base of the rocks alongside the channel.

He could read no farther. The familiar gnawing pain of a new duodenal ulcer was beginning again.

Thinking back to last Friday, he visualized the steaming argument with his wife that night, followed by his storming out of their apartment and vowing never to return. Her transformation from angel to shrew in less than two years of marriage had been remarkable. Now he was relegated to the couch and that was fine with him.

He'd driven to a side street a couple of blocks away from the beach, parked his Range Rover there, then walked to the beach with his ratty old dark gray sleeping bag curled underneath an arm.

Three lifeguard stands, no longer in use for the summer crowds, were lined up close together for the fall and winter months. No one would notice him sacking out on the sand underneath the lifeguard stand that stood in the middle.

He remembered being startled by strange sounds coming from the direction of the jetty. Peeking out from the inner warmth of his sleeping bag, he could make out the silhouette of a man whose loud cackle was high-pitched and exploded in bursts as he walked along the top the jetty.

Roger had watched in terror as the man left the jetty and suddenly broke into a run toward the parking area. Immediately covering his head, he'd lain still until he heard the man driving away. What was that man doing on the jetty so late at night? He'd automatically checked the time. It was ten twenty-two.

Now, as Roger looked again at the photo of the double jetty, he wondered if he should call the police. Wasn't his life complicated enough already without his involvement in this case? Would his information even be helpful?

What would he have to report? The man had broad shoulders, he walked on the jetty with long, fast strides, he had a strange way of laughing, and he left the jetty at ten twenty-two.

But there was something else.

Right before he started to run, the man howled—a long, mournful howl like a coyote. That was what had scared Roger so much he'd lain still and held his breath until the man drove off.

Roger picked up the paper, left Starbucks, and went directly to his Rover. With the windows shut, he spoke into his phone.

21

"Yes, we were all shocked to hear of Tegan Hartwood's death," said Elisa Beckham. "Not only was she one of our very best customers for the past two years, but she appreciated women's shoes as fine art. She always phoned our department before coming in to make sure I was here and by the time she arrived, I would have several selections to her exact taste and needs lined up and ready to start with."

"Did she come in often?" asked Ling, as she slid her right foot into a sling-back pump with color-blocking, peek-a-boo cutouts and a patterned, fish-skin heel.

"Oh my goodness, yes," said the good-natured saleslady. "This was not the only place she shopped, of course, but I'd say she came in about once a month or so. Tegan wanted to breathe in the smells of the shoes, feel their textures, and admire their workmanship, not shop online. We had the best time talking about some of the famous collectors like former Philippines First Lady Imelda Marcos, who had 1,060 pairs.

"And Tegan had her own collection. She would always tell me the latest number after buying a pair here. She was so excited when I brought out those silver heels they talked about on the news. Marina Marison is a young brand that already has enough style and pizazz to compete with decades-old shoemakers. They brought her collection up to 461."

"A formidable number," said Peggy. She took the pair of flats spun of satin and embellished with pearls and crystals out of their box and put them on.

"Not really so surprising. She was, after all, an accomplished artist who could appreciate the unique artistry in many of these shoe designs, fabrics, colors, and

51

shapes," commented Elisa as she swung an arm around to motion toward some of the shoe department displays.

"I heard you're the top salesperson in women's shoes," said Ling.

"It's a world I've happily immersed myself in. As a little girl, the fascination started with Cinderella's glass slippers. Today's girls have Barbie's Louboutins."

"What I want to know is how sex and the shoe ever got established?" Ling inquired.

"Catherine de Medici is said to have invented high heels so she would look more elegant for her wedding in 1533, and Marie Antoinette wore heels as she walked onto a guillotine platform to be executed in 1793. In January of this year, a pair of her high-heeled shoes was on display in an exhibition in Paris. Their fabric had a floral design on a royal blue background. They had open toes and beaded trim all the way around. Surprisingly, they even had ankle straps with large bows in front. She was ahead of her time! But what cemented the sex-shoe relationship was the introduction of the stiletto heel in 1954.

"Women's shoes today have personality plus and are one of the most expedient ways to demonstrate taste. As Marilyn Monroe used to say, 'Give a girl the right pair of shoes and she'll conquer the world.'"

"If only it were as easy as that," Ling laughed lightly. "Do you have my size in those pointy pumps with the three textures?"

"Smart choice," said the saleswoman. "They're leather, suede and on-trend calf hair."

"May I see something with a wedge?" asked Peggy.

"Of course, I have specifically the thing."

As Elisa gingerly walked into the back room, Peggy looked at Ling. "We've got to find out if Tegan confided in her about whom she was seeing."

"I know," answered Ling. "As long as we can keep her talking, we'll be able to smoothly lead up to the right way of ferreting out that information."

When Elisa came back, she was carrying a stack of boxes, three of which she set before Peggy and one in front of Ling.

While Peggy buckled the strap on a pair of wedges, Ling wriggled her feet into the tri-texture pumps and walked over to the mirror to see how they looked.

After chatting for a few minutes about the latest footwear trends, Ling started in. "You must really miss having a customer so knowledgeable about the business you're in. Not too many of us know nearly that much."

"I've been selling shoes for over 20 years," answered Elisa. "And believe me, she was a rarity."

"Tegan was wearing the Marina Marison shoes you helped her select when she was murdered. Who would do such a terrible thing?"

Elisa stared straight ahead, her smile vanished. "She was here a few days before it happened. She was excited about seeing someone who wasn't showing any interest for a while and then, all of a sudden, he was. She said he was coming over to her house for a late dinner last Friday night.

"We had a good laugh together about how young men these days are thoroughly brainwashed to get turned on by certain trendy looks. She said that with the new shoes and her lamé dress, whose fabric was woven with thin ribbons of metallic fiber, he wouldn't stand a chance."

Elisa paused and furrowed her forehead. She looked into the distance and her next words seemed to be addressed to no one in particular.

"I recall how one shoe was slightly loose because her left foot was ever so slightly larger than her right. 'That's all right,' she told me, 'they won't be on for long.'"

"These last wedges you brought out might go with an outfit I have in mind, but I'm not sure this is the right shade of blue," Peggy said, trying not to appear as if they were pushing too hard for information about Tegan.

"Why don't you take them home and see. If they don't work, you're welcome to bring them back," smiled Elisa.

No wonder Tegan always bought her shoes from this saleswoman, thought Peggy, as she handed her charge card to Elisa. A couple of minutes later, Elisa returned for Peggy's signature and handed her a Neiman Marcus department store bag with the shoe box inside.

"It was a pleasure waiting on you ladies," Elisa said. "You know, I have not been able to get Tegan's demise off my mind. It really bothers me that whoever was with her last Friday night so completely fooled her."

"It's very troubling to us too," said Ling "that whoever committed this crime could still be in the area."

"Oh, I feel almost certain that he is," Elisa added.

Peggy and Ling looked at Elisa expectantly.

"One thing Tegan told me quite a while back stuck with me: 'Sea and Shore Fitness is a gold mine for my kind of man.'"

"Tegan's statement certainly makes it pretty reasonable to assume the killer most likely can be found at that fitness center," Peggy said as soon as they got back into Ling's car. Our time here was well spent."

"So will you be putting the gym on your agenda next?'

"It's already on it. Barb's coming along as my guest tomorrow to begin one of their free one-week trial memberships."

"Let me know how you do"

"Will do. What about your feature story? Any particular angle next?"

"Between her vast shoe collection and her watercolor paintings, as well as her penchant for buff men, Tegan is certainly shaping up as a colorful character to write about," said Ling.

Ling grinned as she drove in the direction of the library to drop Peggy off. "That detective could never have pulled this off. He might have the last high heels Tegan ever wore in police custody, true, but we are the ones who tried on shoes for a couple of hours and got Elisa talking, only in the special way that women confide in other women."

"Ling, if Blane Sandingis ever walked into the women's shoe department, with his classic Lithuanian looks and caramel hair, the women would be queueing up like crazy to be questioned."

22

*D*elphinium was curled up on the living room carpet when Ling returned home. "Come on, my forty-five-mile-per-hour sleepy time gal, it's time to get up," she said, patting the Italian greyhound affectionately.

After freshening the dog's water and pouring her favorite crunchy chow into her bowl, Ling pulled the combination of hand-written notes and printed pages from her bedroom desk that she'd composed so far, spread them out on the dining room table, then organized them according to subtopic.

Half an hour later, she fixed herself a salad of mixed greens seasoned with light Italian dressing and goat cheese. Delphinium was especially sensitive to Ling's moods and often climbed up on her lap whenever Ling was down and out. Thankfully, those days were fewer and fewer, thought Ling. And today, she was feeling on a definite roll with her story so Delphinium's ears and tail were at attention.

She had gotten the animal shortly after her divorce and because of the dog's gray-blue coat, named her after the beautiful blue flower that symbolizes ardent attachment and an open heart. In these past two years, Ling and Delphinium had developed a strong bond.

Ling recalled that in selecting a greyhound, she had taken into account that they are easy to take care of. No shedding, no slobbering, no barking, and all they need is a quick wipe-down after a walk and a good run once a week. Besides, they are gentle, loyal, loving, and enjoy the company of people and dogs. Because of those distinctive traits, as well as their sleek structure and elegant lines, the animals appear often in the art of ancient Greece and Rome.

SECRET OF THE JETTY

And Delph is patient to boot, she thought. If I stop to chat with a neighbor during our walks, she stands by me quietly. If it's someone she distrusts, she backs up. But that seldom happens.

As she ate, Ling felt elated. When Mark Evanston gave me this assignment, I thought I'd be on my own for this story, but with Peggy and her friends, I've got three secret assistants.

A couple of hours later, Ling pressed *Send* on her HP laptop and her first installment of "Murder on the Jetty" was on its way to her editor for publication in *Seaside Magazine*'s Wednesday print edition.

"Delph, this calls for a celebration. How about some extra-long play time at Dog Beach next weekend?"

23

"I would like to try your Pilates classes and my guest is more interested in working out on the machines," Peggy told the girl at the front desk as she handed her the free trial coupon, signed herself and Barb in, and then filled out a short form with spaces for place of work, phone number, age, and fitness goals.

"You may have heard we've recently lost one of our two Pilates instructors. Until we hire a replacement, there will be fewer classes available. Some of Tegan's regulars showed up today anyway to at least work out on the machines."

"I heard about it on the news four days ago," responded Peggy. "What a tragic thing to happen! All of you who worked with her must still be in shock."

"We're all reeling from it and so are the regulars who took Tegan's classes."

"Did you know her well?"

"The one who probably knew her best, I mean, besides Milburn—that's the manager—was the other Pilates instructor. Let's see…you're in luck. Becky has a class starting at eleven-thirty. Can you hang around till then or do you want to come back later?"

"That's only a little over an hour from now and with the list of things your ad said there are to do here, I'm sure to find something else to fill in the time."

"I can try to find someone to give you a tour. By the way, my name is Carla."

"That's okay. I'm pretty good at self-guided tours."

"Well, feel free to walk around and get acquainted with us. This is a friendly gym."

That is exactly what I intend to do, thought Peggy.

"I definitely could use a second cup of coffee before working out," said Barb, as they neared the Fit & Slim Café, which was located in an alcove of the gym with room for six tables and chairs.

"Actually, not a bad place to start," said Peggy, as Barb sat down at one of the tables. "I can hang out here with my laptop. Got to get it from the car. Be right back."

While heading toward the front door, Peggy noticed Carla standing alone, seemingly with nothing pressing to do. She waved Peggy over.

"I forgot to mention that one of our trainers will have to show your guest how to properly use all the machines," she said. "So please tell her to let me know when she's ready for her free introductory lesson."

"How long will that lesson be?"

"Only about twenty minutes. After that, she can exercise all she wants."

"It seems fairly quiet today. I guess that's because of what happened to Tegan."

Carla grimaced. "You should have seen it here Monday—some handsome detective and two cops looking all around and asking questions the whole day. A real zoo. We had a sub teaching Tegan's classes. She was pretty shaken up after they barged into each of the classes so they could speak to everyone at once."

"What did the police want to know?"

"Which of our members Tegan might have gone out with last Friday…or used to go out with. They got here real early. I had to pull our men's membership info and make copies for them.

"The young guys here were filing in and out of that extra office next to Milburn's all morning. They were called in one at a time."

"Did they also talk to Becky's eleven-thirty class, the one I'll be in today?"

"Sure, saying stuff like Tegan could have been targeted by a member of Sea and Shore, and if anyone here has even the slightest suspicion of who this man could be to speak up. Before they left, they said they'd be following up with a few of our members. Full cooperation was expected."

"Did they also talk to Milburn and Becky?"

"The detective spoke with each of them separately, before zeroing in on the youngest guys. Milburn was a wreck. Today, he's keeping his office door closed and told me not to disturb him except for an emergency."

"I'm sure it was a tough day for you," Peggy said as the girl turned to greet two new arrivals.

"You've got that right."

"Did you get lost?" Barb asked with a trace of sarcasm when Peggy finally returned to the café with her laptop.

"Guess what I found out? Sandingis was here Monday trying to find out which members of this gym Tegan was currently seeing or had dated in the past. He focused on the men who either took one of her classes or Becky's eleven-thirty class. Two officers also scrutinized the membership list."

Barb chuckled. "Sharp minds think alike. I wonder if Sandingis has lined up any definite suspects yet."

"By the way, the receptionist needs you to come see her before you get started on the machines. Rules."

"It's certainly sad about that instructor,' Peggy said as she paid the café cashier for a vanilla yogurt.

"Oh yes, Tegan, I knew her," answered the white-haired, plump woman behind the counter. "She used to stop by when she had a break in between classes and always got a fruit cup and bottled water."

"What about the manager? Did he come in also?"

"Hardly ever. He ate in his office or went out for lunch. Funny, but last time I saw him in here, Tegan was sitting down over there," she said, pointing at a corner table. "After he noticed her, he sat three tables away and turned his back toward her. He didn't say one word, not even a quick hello"

"How long ago was that?"

"Sometime last month, I guess. I remember it was before Tegan was named Instructor of the Year, which made Milburn's rude behavior toward her even more odd. I mean, why boost Tegan's career like that if they were not even on speaking terms. That's probably why it stuck in my mind."

Peggy sat down with her yogurt, opened her laptop and started to type meaningless gibberish. She was only using the PC as her cover for being there. After a few minutes, she was rewarded for her patience when two 20-something women, flush from exercising, came in and paused before walking up to the counter. It was obvious they were dissing Tegan and in decibel levels high enough so that Peggy didn't have to make any effort to eavesdrop.

"So I'm sorry about what happened, but she was so full of herself. She came onto that good-looking Irish guy with freckles and sandy brown hair, the one who randomly pops in to work out."

"I know. I mean, it was so obvious. She'd be happening to slink by at the exact time he headed for the locker room. I've seen him lifting weights sometimes."

"Word is she had eyes for a couple of the other weightlifters too."

"Like Joe?"

"Yeah. A fab looker."

"My med assistant classes are in the afternoons so I've been able to take the eight o'clock Pilates class on Mondays, Wednesdays, and Fridays. One thing good about Tegan, she sure knew how to teach the right moves."

"True enough. I was taking her ten o'clock sessions, but only once in a while. Come to think of it, a couple of times, that Irish knockout showed up."

The two women ordered, paid the cashier, and left with their smoothies. Peggy closed her computer, smiled at the cashier, and walked toward the women's locker room, making certain to pass by the weightlifting area on the way. The so-called Irish guy wasn't there.

But could any of these other weightlifters have been Tegan's last date? Peggy wondered. Is the one named Joe here now?

24

A skinny 30-something honey blonde with her hair pulled back in a pony-tail, wearing black tights and a fitness center logo top was pulling out a Pilates mat from one of the lockers.

"Hi, I'm trying out the fitness center this week. My name's Peggy. By any chance, are you Becky?"

"Well, welcome, I sure am."

"You've got to be so busy this week with your own class plus Tegan Hart-wood's."

"No way can I take on Tegan's or any other extra classes. I work almost full time as a personal fitness trainer, so my eleven-thirty Pilates class on Mondays, Wednesdays, and Fridays is enough. There are four other instructors who divvy up all the rest of the different kinds of classes held here."

"The receptionist mentioned you and Tegan were friends. I'm so sorry for your loss."

"We got along great here, but I'm married and she wasn't, so we didn't really get together outside of work. Tegan taught her classes earlier in the morning, same days as my class, and afterward she met with her fitness trainees. She was out of here by two o'clock."

"Did she work on any other days?"

"Those three days were enough for her to stay fit and check out the guys. She made more than enough from her paintings, didn't need the extra money. But she did not want to hit the bar scene, thought this was the safest way to scan plenty of men and then pick and choose the ones she wanted. With access to the membership files, she easily discovered their ages, occupations, and home addresses."

"Judging from her photo in the news, she was a real beauty."

"She was a knockout and she knew it." Becky shut her locker door and headed slowly toward the exit.

"Good thing I didn't pick Monday to start my free week, what with the police questioning everyone about whom she dated."

"As I told the detective in charge, Tegan never gave me any names outright. But she sure knew what she was looking for in minute detail."

"Height, weight, and eye color?" asked Peggy.

"Tall, super athletic, great looking, a working brain—college education minimum—and the cutoff age was twenty-nine.

"Pretty picky, huh?"

"For her, it was more than flesh on flesh; it was a mind game too."

"Knowing all those requirements, does anyone in particular stand out as her most probable recent conquest?"

"I can think of a few possibles, but I can't say for sure one is more likely than any other. She always flirted openly with practically all the men, so that way it was anyone's guess who her boyfriend could be at any given time."

Becky looked at the wall clock. "Class is starting in five minutes so we'd better get in there. You know what? Two possibilities will be in my class right now. They were floaters between Tegan's classes and mine, and you'll know them when you see them."

"So was this little escapade worth it or what!" Barb exclaimed as she and Peggy drove off. "Look at my hair. Don't you think I could use some highlights?"

"What?" Peggy looked dumbfounded.

"I am going to go home and make an appointment with Tegan's hairstylist."

"You're kidding. You found out who that is?"

"Anita, owner of Anita's Salon & Spa. And you realize hairstylists know even more than bartenders about their regulars. I can picture Tegan pouring out all her juicy secrets every four weeks for years to the gal who kept her copper tresses silky and Hollywood gorgeous."

"You hope."

"Aren't you going to ask me how I found out?"

"While you were huffing and puffing on the machines, someone next to you happened to say they go to the same salon Tegan went to?"

"Better. I got to chatting with my temp trainer Tony about how tragic Tegan's death was. Told him I saw her picture and how gorgeous she was with her copper blonde hair and cobalt eyes. Pretty soon, he started bragging that he gets his hair done by the same stylist and about how talented she is. Perfect opener for me to ask who."

Peggy nodded. "I couldn't agree more that our time spent here so far has been revealing. The snack bar cashier let it slip that Milburn was not on speaking terms with Tegan and their tiff was going on before he named her Instructor of the Year. Strange, huh?"

"I'll say. Anything else?"

"Uh-huh. I know precisely the kind of men Tegan was interested in and two of them were in the class I just took. Their names are James and Addison. After class, the younger women looked fruitlessly for any chance to buzz around them."

Barb lit up. "If Tegan went for looks, I spotted one amazing guy starting to head toward the weight room as I was on my way to meet you up front. Sandy hair, Irish looks. Maybe she dated him."

"Wait till I tell you what I overheard about that very guy. But Tegan zeroed in on appearance plus so much more than that. I'll fill you in before we come back."

"To do what exactly?"

"Well, to check out James and Addison for one thing. Find a way to talk to them before or after Becky's class."

Peggy was on a roll. "Another thing, we haven't talked to Milburn yet. "My full day off changes weekly. Can you make it back here with me next Monday?"

25

"You've got some awfully tired hair here," Anita announced as she grabbed a handful of Barb's chestnut hair by the ends and held it up high in front of the mirror.

It was ten o'clock Thursday morning. What a way to start the day, thought Barb.

"That's why I'm here," she responded. "Thanks so much for fitting me in."

"Anyone recommended by Tony…and luckily, I had a last-minute cancellation."

After Barb's highlight color was agreed upon, Anita started the procedure, pausing after a few minutes to answer a call.

"Yes," Anita said into the phone, "I can do your cut while my other customer's waiting for her highlights to take."

Uh-oh, this last-minute other customer is going to drastically reduce our chit-chat time, thought Barb. There's no time for a warm-up; I've got to plunge right in.

"When I spoke to Tony yesterday, he was still shell-shocked over Tegan Hartwood's death. The gym was unnaturally quiet."

"I still can't believe it," said Anita. "She was in here exactly one week before some monster left her out on that jetty…so full of energy, a dynamite lady, kept me laughing, telling me how she'd choose her shoes according to her moods. I sure will miss her."

"I heard she lived alone in a big, beautiful beach house."

"Tegan said she had no family. Her parents divorced when she was little and her father was never heard from since. She had no siblings and her mother is dead."

"If only the police can find out which guy she had a date with last Friday night," Barb ventured. "Is there any chance she might have dropped some clue about him?"

"I've been racking my brain. The last time I did her hair she was looking forward to a romantic date coming up that following Friday. She didn't describe the man at all."

"What about in the not too distant past? Did she ever say anything specific about a man in her life?"

"No, she'd say general things like she was as careful about choosing her men as she was about choosing her shoes. But I do remember she had me in stiches about some hot man who should have never been a priest at St. Michael's. I thought it was a joke."

"About how long ago was that?"

"About two appointments back, so a little more than two months ago."

26

"*Three, two, one,*" Samantha Winterly was one of those TV news reporters the camera loved, no matter how serious her expression or grave her tone. And she was always ready the instant the camera clicked on.

"I'm not going out on a limb at all to say that, based on the glamorous way Tegan Hartwood was attired—silver dress and shoes—at the time her body was found on a Carlsbad jetty last Friday, she had to have been on a date that moonlit night.

"With no husband and, as yet, no known love interest at the time of her demise, this could prove to be a particularly baffling case. No life insurance policy and no will were left behind by the victim, although she was very wealthy. Police are continuing to search for a strong motive that possibly will lead to the perp."

Ling clicked off the Thursday noon news report with a triumphant smile. There's no way Samantha could have known how Tegan was dressed unless she read my story in the magazine yesterday, she thought.

27

Right after Peggy received Barb's text, she told the other reference librarian she'd be back as soon as she made an important call. It was twelve forty-five. Outside of the library, she speed-dialed Ling.

"Ling, this is Peggy. I'm at work now but listen, I heard from Barb a couple of minutes ago. She got a tip from Tegan's hair stylist this morning that there's a good chance Tegan might have had some sort of involvement with a priest at Saint Michael's."

"This case keeps getting better."

"We don't know his name but most Catholic parishes these days have no more than two full-time priests. To meet Tegan's criteria, he'd have to be the younger priest, no older than twenty-nine, tall, handsome, athletic. *Smart* would be a given. Do you think you could come up with a reason for interviewing him?"

"Mmm. How about I'm doing a story on the Catholic Church's push to attract slackers back into the fold?

"I know a few Taiwanese women who belong to Saint Michael's so it won't be difficult to dig up some facts about the church before I ask the priest if he has a 15-minute slot for an interview some time before Sunday."

"This has potential."

"Peggy, I'm going to text you as soon as I have the interview scheduled."

28

As soon as she pressed the key fob to lock her Toyota, Peggy's attention was drawn upward to several nylon and polyester kites dancing rhythmically in the wind, their bright, full range of colors popping against the baby blue sky. As she walked from the parking area toward the jetty, her eyes and her smile caught those of a young couple who, it turned out, were celebrating the husband's birthday by surfing and picnicking on the wide South Ponto beach.

"I'm surprised there are a few surfers out with the waves so rough," Peggy remarked.

"Oh, we surfers know to go past the *white* to the *mother* and then catch a wave and ride it horizontally down the coast, south of the jetties," the husband explained in a friendly tone.

"Between the two jetties, there's a strong undertow during high tide that would carry someone down to the lagoon."

Peggy thought about the body on the jetty that had been cradled so safely by the rocks. She had purposely arrived at the jetty half an hour before her friends while the tide was still low. She walked across the rocks and started working her way down to the rock upon which Tegan had lain and died. She hoped spending quiet time in the crime scene atmosphere would help her concentrate on the case, maybe even spark an intuitive hunch.

The grinning fisherman on the jetty across from her, fixated on watching an eddy starting to form at the tip of the south jetty and imagining wide-open bites, paid no attention as she kneeled down and lightly ran her hands across the rocks that had surrounded Tegan.

Had these rocks absorbed the evil emotions of the killer and the terrified feelings of the victim? Did they still hold those negative energies? What words were spoken here? If only the jetty could communicate its secret.

Peggy swung around to a sitting position. The man who had committed this crime surely was a tortured soul and he made certain Tegan became such a soul before she died. But if she'd lived, Tegan eventually might have turned the corner on her lifestyle and realized how empty her life was with no meaningful connections. Now we'll never know, she thought.

A sudden chill ran down her spine. Were the rocks of the jetty crying out?

Looking at her watch, Peggy climbed back to the top of the jetty. Now, at a few minutes after nine, her friends joined her.

29

"It was exactly one week ago that we stood here, never dreaming in our wildest imaginations that we'd discover a crime scene," said Peggy.

"I for one will never feel the same about this jetty, or any other jetty for that matter," Barb admitted.

Cassie looked down the side of the jetty to the rock where Tegan had been lying. The sea water in the lagoon pushed and pulled dark seaweed, forcing it to sway back and forth. The same frightened feeling she had experienced last Saturday suddenly flowed through her body.

Silently, the three women filed down to the beach and began walking southward.

"Look," said Peggy, "the police will solve this case—eventually. But they can't be expected to do every single nit-picky extra thing that we're able to accomplish."

She suppressed a smile. "Actually, we can do more in some ways. At least, we don't have to read people their rights before questioning them. And we can go ahead and call any and all suspicious men suspects; the police have to be careful to call them persons of interest.

"So meanwhile, let's keep on forging ahead to help move the investigation along. We've only got a few days at best before someone figures out who we are and our names get out there.

"Barb, you and I are all set to hit the gym again Monday, and Cassie, can you get down to that art gallery in La Jolla that carries Tegan's paintings?"

"First thing on tomorrow's to-do list," said Cassie. "They're open noon till four on Sundays."

"And by Wednesday, the three of us really need to check out Tegan's house to get a feel for how she lived, maybe even talk to her next-door neighbors. That's something Ling would want to be in on too. Today, she's interviewing Father Stevens so she and I will be in touch anyway."

"Finding out about that priest while at Anita's Salon was a terrific tip," Barb said.

"Definitely. We also know that James and Addison were Tegan's type, and that there was an ongoing cold war between Milburn and Tegan still evident three weeks before the murder."

"Oh, how I wish I were going to the fitness center with you two on Monday," Cassie sighed. "You're picking up clue after clue there."

The three women picked up their pace, passing tide pools that revealed various species of algae, acorn barnacles, anemones, sea stars and shore crabs. Wavelets rippled into the shoreline, angled at different degrees from the much larger horizontal wave lines, some even perpendicular to them.

"What can we say at this point regarding motive?" asked Cassie.

"Well, nobody's gaining any wealth by her demise so money's out. Also, there was no evidence of intimacy," Peggy pronounced.

"A moment of passion during an argument, sudden rage, was always out," murmured Cassie.

Barb was emphatic. "Absolutely right. This was meticulously planned. The killer did not throw her down on the rocks. There was nothing gruesome about this murder, no blood and guts, no violent physical action by the killer. Natural forces took her life."

"Helped along by a serving of hemlock," Peggy quickly added.

"Jealousy?" pressed Cassie.

"No reason at all for that," said Barb. "Anita told me Tegan would come to the salon and wax enthusiastic about one boyfriend at a time—no names. That could go on for months. Each guy would be the only one in the picture only until the day she suddenly decided to drop him, so the killer would not have had any other guy to be overwhelmingly jealous of."

"Because each and every guy would inevitably meet the same fate as the one before him," explained Peggy.

"Mmm, let's not dismiss jealousy so fast," said Cassie. "What if Tegan broke her usual pattern and decided, just one time, to cheat on her current flame? What if her lifestyle was not quite enough for her anymore? Maybe she scratched her itch and he found out."

Peggy was quick to respond. "She'd never have needed two men at the same time. According to Becky, the second Tegan was not fully and entirely satisfied with a guy, she'd move on with no hesitation."

"I still say she might have initiated a one-nighter with someone brand new who was not even connected to the gym," Cassie mused, as the friends circled around a couple of teenagers playing Frisbee.

This mystery is like an orchestra with all its discordant, disconnected sounds as it warms up before a performance, Peggy thought. Then she asked, "Have either of you considered revenge as a possible motive?

"The desire for revenge seems to be a natural impulse. There was an article in *National Geographic* years ago about the ancient Romans writing petitions to deities to inflict revenge. They'd etch grievances into thin lead sheets and bury them in tombs or throw them into wells. More than fifteen hundred have been found so far."

Ever the English teacher, Cassie pounced on the moment to quote Shakespeare. "'If you harm me, shall I not revenge?' *Merchant of Venice.*"

"What I think," answered Barb, "is we're looking for someone patient, methodical, with a logical mind, determined—a man with a seething hatred that metastasized into rage. It all starts with hurt, you realize. Maybe in the killer's mind, this was the only way to right a grievous wrong.

"When my hospitalized patients who were chronically angry opened up, they'd always refer to an injustice—or at least a perceived injustice—that had been done to them earlier in their lives or that was currently being done. They also were the patients who had the longest and toughest recoveries from illness or operations."

Cassie resumed her theme, but with a fresh angle. "How about a new lover with extreme rage at Tegan's lifestyle? Every now and then, there is something in the news about a serial killer who's obsessed about ridding the world of a certain type of woman he despises," she said, shuddering at the thought.

"At least," said Barb, "there haven't been any such maniacal killings around here."

"So far," said Cassie, "but they all start somewhere."

"Hopefully not in this case," added Barb.

By now, they had reached Moonlight Beach in Encinitas and turned around to head back to their starting point. Large brown patches of floating seaweed, a few surfers, and a kayak caught Peggy's eye as she glanced toward the greyish-green ocean. The surf played its eternal game: waves rolling in on shore 26 to the minute, in all kinds of weather. She watched, as one white cap broke on the sand, dissolved into its own foam, then rapidly retreated under the crest of an oncoming wave.

Peggy added to the list of questions they were batting back and forth. "Could she have been a threat to the killer in some way? Blackmail?"

Barb reiterated her position with increased emphasis. "No, no. Then he could have simply poisoned her and let it go at that. Why this elaborately staged murder? His M.O. was extremely personal."

"So the motive could be two-fold: blackmail plus something else," Cassie threw out.

"Actually, someone could be extremely angry about being blackmailed, especially if it is open-ended, and the blackmailer keeps upping the demands," said Peggy.

"The killer could have been enraged by any number of things. His mistake was allowing anger to lodge within himself and grow to the point of ruining his own life as well as his victim's," Barb added.

This case is like the tangled 14-foot kelp strewn on the beach after a storm, thought Peggy, as she and her friends continued striding along the water's edge in silence for the next few minutes. Aware of kelp bulbs popping under her weight, she looked down. The khaki sand was interspersed with gray-black smudges that made it look as if a tractor had traversed it recently.

Then, true to her habit of summing up their various viewpoints after a long walk and talk, she spoke. "I agree this murder was well-planned and carried out in a deliberate, calculating, fastidiously careful manner. What we must ask ourselves is: Why did he want her to die in this specific way? She had to lie there knowing every time seawater washed across that rock, her vulnerability to drowning increased and there was nothing she could do but lie there in horror, paralyzed."

"Whatever his reason for hating Tegan so intensely, he made sure he had complete power over her at the end," Cassie agreed.

"Of course, our killer might have already been a disturbed person, way before he even met Tegan," Barb mused.

"Then he's not only smooth and crafty," concluded Peggy, but he's still a danger to the community."

30

"*How* good it is to meet you, Father Steven. Thank you for seeing me this afternoon."

Ling entered the rectory, shook the priest's hand, sat down on the sofa directly across from him, and placed her notepad and pen on the coffee table. She was making mental checkmarks next to the words *tall, handsome, young.* She also noted that his facial features lived up to his Irish last name, Caffrey.

"I understand that all the pews are full during Masses here at Saint Michael's," she started. "Nevertheless, I know the Catholic Church is concerned about those who have fallen away. Obviously, you are doing something very right to attract and keep your parishioners."

"Attendance at Mass has increased since we started our in-depth studies three years ago. Participants are encouraged to ask questions and we love answering them. The more our congregation understands Catholicism, the more they want to follow its teachings.

"Many churches keep their doors locked except for Masses and I don't blame them. But our older parishioners miss the days when they could stop by during the week to light a candle and enjoy some quiet time with God. Our doors stay open on Tuesdays and Fridays until four o'clock."

"You're certainly doing all you can to accommodate your parishioners. What about donations to your school fund this year? Sources tell me you've had some big donors."

"We have been blessed in this way."

"Was Tegan Hartwood one of them?" Ling watched Father Steven's face closely as he prepared to respond.

He rummaged through his hair. "Why yes, she was most generous. I see that word gets around. Terrible about her death." The priest's eyes broke contact for a few seconds but his voice remained even.

"It took a cruel and evil man to abandon her on that jetty." Ling added.

Father Steven looked at his watch and rose from his chair, a clear signal that their time was up.

"Thank you again," said Ling. "Father, I can't help but ask. You look like someone who works out regularly. Is it possible you are a member of Sea & Shore Fitness Center?"

Father Stevens cracked his first smile. "You've caught me."

Ling put a mental checkmark next to the word *athletic* and left.

Father Steven Caffrey's stomach started hurting again.

The reason Ling Chen gave for this meeting was a cover, he thought. Her true purpose was to investigate any connection between Tegan Hartwood and me. This journalist has the potential power to ruin my religious career, my vocation—simply by implying in print that there was something between us. I would have to leave the priesthood and give up my ministries, my purpose in life.

There's only one way out of this: something has to shift her focus onto someone else.

31

$\mathcal{B}$y five o'clock Saturday afternoon, Peggy put in a call to Ling.

"I was about to ring you too, Peggy. You won't believe this, but you can add Father Steven Caffrey to our list of suspects."

"What? Why?" Peggy could visualize the writer's satisfied facial expression at the other end of the phone line.

"He knew Tegan. She dropped off boxes of toys and classroom supplies for the parochial school to the rectory, where he lives. To top this off, Father Steven is known as Steve at Sea & Shore Fitness, where he keeps up his strength by lifting weights. This fits in with our belief that the perp's most likely someone from the gym."

"Hah! How much do you want to bet she dropped her donations off on a dark and sultry evening? Did you take his picture?"

"I'd have been careless to miss the chance."

"Good," said Peggy. "If you print a copy, I'll show your photo to Barb before we start sleuthing around the gym again on Monday. Father Steven—Steve— could be the man she noticed heading toward the weight room the first time we were there. Sandy brown hair?"

"Sandy brown as it can be."

Peggy shifted gears. "Ling, can you squeeze in a visit to Tegan's house next Wednesday? By then, the police will be finished there, don't you think?"

"I'll put it on my schedule. Seeing how she lived will certainly help round out my story."

Peggy laughed. "I can hear Sandingis now, 'What do you ladies think you're going to discover in this house that my team has not already found?'"

"When we put our four heads together and add up everything we will have figured out by the end of this week, he's going to be one amazed detective."

Turning introspective, Peggy added, "I feel a sense of responsibility, as if I'm being pulled forward more and more into this case to know who Tegan really was. Maybe the better I know her, the closer I'll get to figuring out who murdered her and why."

"So far, she doesn't measure up as a very savory character."

"Unfortunately, that's true. But no matter what the victim was like, no one has the right to be judge and executioner."

"Agreed. And yet, she had to have done something horrendous…"

"Something that could make a man want to first poison and then abandon her to the murderous whims of nature."

Ling paused. "You should know I will finally be interviewing Sandingis on Tuesday."

"Great. What are you going to wear?" Peggy teased.

Ling couldn't help but grin. "Come on, Peg, this will be a significant interview, vital to the integrity of my story."

"That aside, you've got to admit he'd be one tantalizing catch."

His face flashed before her: chiseled features, prominent jawline, high cheekbones, caramel hair and amber eyes. His apparel was a perfect balance of polished and casual: layered tops, slim-fit pants, and burnished mid-brown leather boots with rubber soles.

"Uh huh, sure, a *Beauty and the Beast* tale with the genders reversed. He's far too handsome and I'm way too plain. He must be used to dating stunners." Ling shrugged off the possibility and was about to change the subject.

Peggy couldn't believe her new friend. "You've got to be kidding, Ling. You're a natural beauty."

After a few minutes more of catching up with Ling, Peggy put aside her phone and ruminated in the stone quiet of the study. I never have to wonder if I'm the right match for Mack, and he for me, she knew.

Mack was out playing tennis, his favorite form of exercise. Since retiring as an accountant, he had become an impressive fix-it-upper, who also enjoyed doing a daily stock market analysis.

Her husband was the love of her life and that was dramatically brought home to her last year when she had been tempted by the possibility of romance with an old boyfriend from way back during her college days. But that lure was ephemeral. In his own special way, Mack had let her know that no other man could come close to his deep love and utter devotion to her.

She'd run into Trent at her alumni reunion in Indiana. They had talked for hours, picking up where they left off a lifetime ago. She was semi-shocked when passionate longings were reignited. So when he sent a text letting her know he would be in San Diego the following month for a stockholders meeting and asked if they could meet for lunch, she knew it was time to consult her closest friends.

Barb and Cassie verbalized, and thus reinforced, what she knew deep down inside. We all look back on our lives now and then and wonder what would have happened if we had taken a different path. Yet that different path would have led to other issues and multiple unknowns. In the heat of passion, we can accept someone into our lives we ordinarily would not give the time of day to. Peggy only knew the boyfriend who used to be—in a different place, in a different time, under different circumstances. Whom had he evolved into?

Then along came Mack's email, out of the blue. He had sent it during a lunch break at a three-day financial seminar he was attending. There was no way he could have known about Trent and yet, he must have sensed something. It didn't matter how or what Mack knew; all that mattered were his words.

Dearest Peggy,

I love you with my whole heart and mind and soul and strength.

Mack

Mack had attended the same college but was two years ahead of Peggy. She had a choice back then between Trent and Mack, and she chose Mack.

Now, magically and wonderfully, she found herself falling in love with her husband all over again.

Now that Cassie's with Nicholas, all three of us have happy marriages, Peggy thought. Cassie Harrison was dumped by an errant husband several years ago and vowed to stay single and free. But when she decided to take up line dancing in June of last year, destiny collided with her defensive stance. Losing focus as the dance steps were called out, Cassie suddenly spun around in the wrong direction and grapevined right smack into the midsection of the man directly behind her—whom she married a few months ago. The two of them enjoy referring to their initial meeting as *love at first impact.*

Barb Demeter's husband Drew, who used to run a PR firm, could provide copy for the top stand-up comedians. Barb often quotes his hilarious quips and says his sense of humor propels her forward. There was one unusually hot, humid summer day when Barb returned home from food shopping and was shocked at the high temperature inside of their house. "It's as hot as a mausoleum in here! You should have at least opened some windows when you decided to shut the AC," she complained. Drew calmly quipped, "It's a preview of coming attractions."

Peggy's thoughts soon returned to the case. The community wants to breathe a sigh of collective relief, to know this murderer is not remaining at large. Our special touch is needed to ferret out the kind of information the police would not even consider procuring in our unique manner. Women's brains have more connectivity between the two hemispheres. That's why we women have better multitasking and social skills.

Well, the police have got their methods, we've got ours.

32

"I understand you carry some of Tegan Hartwood's work. May I see it?" asked Cassie.

The artist on Sunday duty at the gallery in La Jolla smiled broadly. "Of course, follow me."

There, hanging in a separate alcove, were four stunning watercolors of the ocean at different times of the day.

"She had an enormous amount of talent. Her work continues to sell at asking prices despite how the current economy has affected art sales in general. There is such an intensity and excitement in them. Now her paintings will be in even greater demand. You do know about her recent demise?"

Cassie couldn't imagine a more perfect opening for the questions she wanted to ask. "Oh, yes, in fact I'm hoping you can tell me a little more about her. You see, I was one of the women who discovered her body on the jetty. Since that horrid experience, I've been trying to help the police piece together as much as possible about Tegan's life and personality."

"Unfortunately, the police will be removing these paintings soon, and they will become part of her estate while it is determined whether someone has a legal claim to them," the artist, a pleasant woman in her thirties, explained.

Starting to lead Cassie across the room, she continued. "These other paintings are grouped separately because, other than the ocean alone, they zero in on little points of interest.

Although Tegan no longer had time to run marathons with all their rules and schedules, she loved to run freely along the beach at days end, stopping to snap photos that might inspire a future painting."

Pointing to each painting as she spoke, the artist said, "This one emphasizes Sanderlings scurrying about, this next one plays up the patterns created in the sea immediately after a wave has crashed, and here we have receding wavelets revealing sand patterns that look like a quilted bedspread. This last scene details various kinds of seashells, like conches, scallops, whelks, cockles, and angel wings in the pinks, oranges, purples, yellows, and blues of a spectacular SoCal sunset.

"About Tegan as a person, I can say she was fun-loving and did not want to ever get into a serious, long, sustained relationship.

"I clearly recall one time when she brought in a new painting, and I invited her to lunch across the street. I inquired how she was so productive, consistently turning out amazing works of art.

"Tegan's eyes kind of glazed over like she was in a trance. She replied that there was a moment a long time ago when she decided what she wanted out of life, and that she would not allow anything or anyone to get in her way to enjoy painting, running, and men.

"We laughed about the men part. I told her I certainly liked men too, but I'd finally found a keeper several years ago. How could I ever forget what she said next?"

Cassie involuntarily held her breath while looking at the artist expectantly.

"'Eventually, they're all throwaways. I've got no time or patience for sentimentality.' That said, Tegan was a great encourager to other artists. She invited everyone connected with this gallery, employees as well as artists with work on display, to sumptuously catered dinners at her home. And I heard from a lady who has purchased more than one of Tegan's paintings that she also threw parties where all of her clients could get to know each other and talk art."

After thanking the artist for her time, Cassie walked briskly to her car. As she drove, she thought that Tegan's redeeming side, although good, still did not assuage her extreme selfishness. She never let anyone interfere with her freedom.

Maybe that was too frustrating for someone.

33

*T*rue to her plan to scope the gym again on Monday, Peggy arrived with Barb just as Becky's eleven-thirty class was finishing and everyone was eager to shower and change. As Barb immediately headed for the weightlifting area, Peggy walked straight to the café. Ten minutes later, luck was about to play out as she hoped.

Unwrapping her organic 73 percent cacao, super-dark chocolate bar, Peggy conversed with the café lady as the two Pilates class suspects from last time entered and sat down at a table right away, instead of first approaching the counter to place their orders.

"Oh, I'm sorry. I shouldn't be talking so loud. My voice must have carried. I hope I didn't upset you more than you already must be about the unbelievable news," said Peggy.

"It was definitely a shock," said the auburn-haired looker. "Say, weren't you in Becky's class last Wednesday? Are you new?"

"I'm here on the special promo," explained Peggy. "Did you know Tegan well?"

"Sometimes I would get up in time for one of Tegan's early morning Pilates classes—if I wasn't working too late the previous night at my restaurant—otherwise I'd catch Becky's later class as I did today. Tegan related to all of us while she was teaching. It almost felt like a private lesson at times. By the way, I'm Addison and this is James. And you are?"

"Peggy. Glad to meet you both. How about you, James? Did you know her well?"

"Yeah, no, not really. I only made it to one of Tegan's classes now and then."

"Oh, you were mostly in Becky's?"

"That's right," James said. "I usually give myself an extra-long lunch break for Becky's Monday, Wednesday, and Friday Pilates classes, grab a quick snack and leave. Once in a while, I work out on the machines."

"When you guys get into the locker room, I'm sure you gab the same way we women do while changing back into our street clothes," Peggy smiled. "Did you ever happen to hear if Tegan was recently involved with anyone here?"

"Only the usual talk about how she was a cougar and would drop her boyfriends without any warning. Nobody actually fessed up to dating her, at least not when I was around," added Addison.

James shifted in his chair. "There's a Steve something who comes in mainly to lift weights, rarely does Pilates, hits the shower, and leaves. Word got around he was down in the dumps after a spin around with her."

"When was that?"

James made a brushing away gesture with his right hand. "I didn't exactly write down the date. It was none of my business, but maybe about a month or two ago."

"That would have been pure speculation," Addison jumped in. Who the heck is spreading stories like this around anyway?"

James kept a poker face. "I'm just saying."

Addison's thick auburn eyebrows had become semaphores in an attempt to explain away his emotional reaction to the locker room gossip. "Tegan never openly held obvious one-on-one long conversations with her boyfriends. She was much smoother than that. Anyway, there's at least one other weightlifter who keeps to himself. I saw him eyeing her a couple of times."

Peggy looked directly at James. She was not about to let on that she already knew all about good old Steve. "Is the one named Steve here today?"

"No, I haven't seen him as much lately."

Now Peggy watched Addison's expression closely as she asked, "What about the other guy?"

Addison looked worried. "He usually drops by around now. Deep brown hair, always in a tank top, you can't miss him."

"Does he have a name?"

"Joe."

The two men abruptly got up and walked toward the counter to order.

Peggy went back to her table, sat down, and started typing, hoping it would appear natural for her to continue conversing with them when they returned.

Both men wanted the focus off themselves as suspects and had gone out of their way to direct her attention elsewhere. Addison had been defensive of Steve, yet wanted her to know about Joe. Her investigative instincts were on high alert but she would have to be very careful at this delicate juncture.

Cocking her head to one side to seem friendly, and in her most jovial tone of voice, Peggy asked the thin-ice question.

"Okay, so which one of you was Tegan seeing?"

James looked down at the turkey burger getting cold on his plate.

Addison was snappy. "Look, I don't know what exactly leaked out, or how, but that was over way back, several months ago. Tegan was never one to kiss and tell. If you are inferring I was her current attraction, you are way off base."

Peggy noted that Addison's worried look had evolved into a fearful one. Pressing her luck, she asked, "Who then?"

"Like I said, you couldn't tell who she was seeing or which guy she was inviting over to her house. She had the kind of body language that flirted with everyone the same way. It was what she did. She never told anyone, and whoever the guy was, he wasn't talking. Why don't you ask Milburn or Becky? They were thick as molasses with Tegan."

Not lately, light-sped across Peggy's mind.

Addison's facial muscles tightened as he folded his arms across his muscular chest. "Who are you anyway, some private investigator? You remind me of some of the smooth, outwardly friendly newspaper food critics who pose as regular customers in my restaurant, but who are really there looking for any flaws or slip-ups."

Peggy closed her PC and pulled the cord from the wall outlet. This was as much as she was going to get from these two for now. As she left the café, she spotted Becky chatting with Tony. When they finished, she would try to grab the instructor for a few quick questions.

While she waited, she made a couple of mental notations. Addison was afraid and resentful, probably because it had gotten around the gym that he had dated Tegan. Addison would need some further scrutiny but at least he had not put on some cool, calm act in the café. He'd let his feelings show.

In stark contrast, the question put before James, the one about dating Tegan, had met with stone silence. Why? Another thing, the shoes he had changed into were ultra-stylish, over-the-top expensive loafers. Had Tegan, the shoe aficionado, recommended them to this much younger, still impressionable man?

34

I might as well get on one of the treadmills for a few minutes so I look busy getting fit like everyone else, Peggy thought. Not only that, but on my way there, I'll pass by the weight room and see how Barb is faring.

It looked as if a man three times Barb's size was showing her weightlifting 101 techniques. Barb's mission was serious but her awkward movements were an amusing sight. Of course I wouldn't look so elegant in the weight room either, Peggy had to chuckle to herself.

By this time, Becky had finished talking with Tony and was striding toward the machine area, probably to meet with one of her trainees. She smiled as she recognized Peggy walking toward her from the opposite direction. "Well, what do you think of our gym so far?"

"Actually, I do prefer a smaller gym like this, rather than the mega ones where you get swallowed up. There's something here for everyone."

Trying to appear nonchalant, she ventured, "By the way, Becky, I noticed that there are photos of all the instructors and trainers hanging on the wall in the hallway. But I didn't see one of Tegan. Surprising, especially since she was Instructor of the Year."

"Oh, there *was* a collage consisting of four photos in a beautiful frame to honor her. It hung there for a good three weeks, until news of her death, and then Milburn immediately told Carla to take it down. Too bad you didn't see it. A copy of the same glam shot Milburn sent out to local media was in it, along with other photos that touted her achievements as a runner. In the earliest photo of her, way back when she was a track star in college, she looked completely different, not at all attractive."

Becky laughed. "Anyone looking at that color picture of her holding a trophy could have thought the other photos were of a totally different person."

"I'd enjoy seeing all the photos. Do you know where they are now?"

"Carla would know. I'm sure she'll be happy to show them to you."

"That would be great. Thanks for everything, Becky. Take care."

"You too. I hope you decide to join us"

Four minutes later, Peggy realized what else she should ask Carla before Milburn returned.

The receptionist was xeroxing some papers. Peggy took a huge gamble and plunged right in. "I heard Tegan and Milburn were an item at one time."

"Wow! People sure like to gossip around here," Carla acknowledged. Lowering her voice to a conspiratorial whisper, she continued, "I have no idea how far things went, but I do remember that Tegan came back to the center one night as I was getting ready to leave for the day. She said she had to talk to Milburn about something important. When I left, the place was empty except for the two of them."

Pay dirt, thought Peggy. "I gather that was unusual."

"Considering that Tegan only worked till two o'clock and never ever came back to the gym afterward except for that one time, I'd say it was. That's why I recall it clearly," Carla explained.

"Do you also recall how long ago that was?"

"About half a year ago." More pay dirt.

"I'd love to see the photos of Tegan that used to be in the hallway. Are they handy?"

"Milburn never said what I should do with them so I took the photos out of their frame and put them away in his office."

"I need to see Milburn before I leave today anyway. If I ask to see them, will he know where they are?"

"For all he knows, I could have thrown them away. He has never referred to them. Let him know I told you they're in the promo drawer, way in the back."

It will be a relief to see how Tegan looked when she was younger, and replace that bloated, wrinkled image of her face and closed eyes I've had in my mind since finding her dead, Peggy thought. Those photos also will fill in some background on how she lived until recently. In the process of learning more about her, I'm bound to stumble on a clue or two.

Carla looked up as Milburn, returning from an extended lunch hour, sailed through the front door. "Hi, boss, one of our prospective members would like to see you."

"Fine. Come on in," he said, extending his hand to Peggy for a firm shake and then leading the way into his office.

35

The trainer who had demoed rudimentary moves for Barb handed her his card. "Three months with me and you'll be solid as a rock. It'll be good-bye saggy skin."

Thanks a lot for that, thought Barb, I'm not *that* saggy.

As soon as the instructor left, Barb silenced her phone for good reason. A very young man, about six-one with bulging biceps, thick, deep brown hair, and a light olive complexion was about to enter the room, and she didn't want to be disturbed. He was wearing a tank top.

Could this be the weightlifter named Joe that Peggy had mentioned? He went straight to the large weights and immediately started his routine.

The only chance I'll have to engage him in conversation will be when he stops to grab a heavier barbell, Barb knew. When the moment came a few minutes later, she was ready.

"Thanks for not laughing at me," she said, looking straight into his dark brown eyes. "Will I ever be able to lift more than three pounds?"

"Keep at it and you will."

"By the way, I'm Barb."

"Joe."

"I'm thinking of joining up here, but the atmosphere is kind of gloomy. Everyone's bummed about Tegan Hartwood's death, I guess. Did you know her?"

"It was impossible for anyone here not to know her."

Barb's window of time was almost up. Muscle man was about to resume his regimen. She tossed the bait.

"I get the idea Tegan was a carefree spirit, didn't want to be restricted by any personal connections."

"She made her choices."

"I heard the police will be focusing on only a few of the men they already interviewed when they were here last Monday, the ones who met each and every one of Tegan's requirements."

"You mean she had a checklist?"

"Sure did."

Joe shrugged. "They've got their job to do. But they'll be wasting their time when they get around to me."

"What a horrible way for Tegan to die," Barb said clearly enough that two other lifters shot glances her way.

"Hey, forty-five minutes here is my only break from the world of computers."

"They keep you hopping."

His eyes cut away from her. "I keep myself hopping. I own the business."

With the desired barbell in hand, Joe walked back to the bench and resumed his routine.

36

James had made a quick stop in the men's room before leaving the gym. By the time he reached the parking lot, Addison's car was already gone. Walking toward his own car, he removed his phone from his jacket pocket after the second ring.

"James, listen," Addison's voice was strained. James could hear the familiar sounds of traffic as his friend drove.

"If anyone asks you about Tegan and me, I hope you recall I was not in any way open to starting to see her again. When she dropped me, I wasn't angry. I knew her reputation. We both moved on, no hard feelings. As you know, I found someone else and completely stopped paying attention to her."

"Don't worry, buddy."

"Thanks, James."

After the call ended, Addison could not stop dwelling on his four-month affair with Tegan until he reached his restaurant, and then again, off and on, for the rest of the day. Truth be told, way back then, he had fallen hard for her.

Tegan was much more than sexy, he remembered. She was smart, talented, exciting, and fun. Best of all, she was adventuresome enough to try out my most creative recipes before I decided whether or not to add them to the dinner menu. I would bring a new dish over to her house, she'd rate it on a scale of one to ten, then we'd talk and talk about adding or subtracting this or that ingredient.

I always knew one day she would decide our time together was up. Sure, I secretly wanted to get back with her for a while. Funny thing, though, I was able to get my act together faster than I originally thought would be possible.

In fact, as time went on, my attraction to her subsided to the point that she actually turned me off. And then, it was too late.

37

"So you're ready to join Sea & Shore? If you let me know which of our activities you're most interested in, I'm certain I can put together an extremely attractive package." Milburn stacked some of the loose flyers and advertising circulars into a neat pile on his desk, then picked up a pen to make notes.

"I still have a few more days before deciding, but I would have to say your state-of-the-art workout machines as well as the Pilates classes would certainly give me the kind of exercise I'm looking for.

"Incidentally, I'm so sorry about what happened to your other instructor. Buzz has it that the police suspect someone here might have been responsible."

Milburn stopped writing and put down his pen. "That's the kind of loose talk that can hurt a good and decent business." Peggy made a mental note of Milburn's habit of opening and closing his right hand in rapid succession unless he had something in it.

"Did Tegan have any enemies you know of?"

"Enemies is too strong a term, but James Anderson was always wise-cracking about her. Big boobs, no heart, that sort of talk. A couple of my ambitious staffers were jealous when she was honored as our Instructor of the Year. But for someone at Sea & Shore to have actually harmed her—no."

"Since she was only a part-time employee, why did you choose her over all the others as the winner?"

"She deserved the honor. Her classes were always full and we received constant compliments from her fitness trainees." Milburn stilled his right hand by holding a notebook.

"When did your fitness center members first find out about Tegan's honor?"

"That's easy. September 20. On that day, any members who were here couldn't have missed the big splash we set up early that day in the hallway. The media received our press kit the same morning."

"Which of her photos did you select for the media?"

"Only the most current one, a close-up she wanted us to use." His voice sharpened. "What on earth has this got to do with anything, and why do you want to know?"

"Mr. Malawsky, I'm certain you want to clear the good name of Sea & Shore from any and all implication of involvement in Tegan's murder as soon as possible. Tegan's award was made known exactly three weeks before she was murdered."

"Yeah, so?"

"Don't you see?" Peggy paused. "That was about the right amount of time needed to carry out the highly detailed plan for her demise."

"Oh, come on, you're actually suggesting a link between the award and the murder?" Still clutching his notebook, Milburn slowly rose from his chair and stood ramrod straight.

"You're really stretching here, lady." As he started to move toward Peggy, he accidentally bumped into the side of his desk "I see you are here merely to pump me for information."

"I'm only a concerned member of this community who wants to help find Tegan's killer as I would think you want to do also, especially since she was your top instructor. On the news, you said you were saddened by her death."

"What else does our magnanimous prospective member want to know that could possibly be helpful to Sea & Shore?" His tone had become sarcastic.

"Let's see. Shall I bring it up?"

Milburn put down his notebook. "No sense in playing shy now."

"You and Tegan weren't getting along, not even on speaking terms when you gave her the title. Why was that?"

Milburn snorted. "You have a lot of nerve coming in here today and making your insinuations."

"I see you're wearing a wedding ring. Was Tegan threatening your marriage in some way?"

As he approached Peggy, Milburn's eyes narrowed and his face reddened. His right hand was involuntarily opening and closing.

"Never mind," said Peggy. "I think I have my answer." She spun around and opened the door.

"I want you and your guest to leave my center—*now*. And you both can forget about ever becoming members."

"Oh, good! Have it *our* way!" answered Peggy. She strutted out of the office, closing Milburn's door behind her. Before exiting, she made sure to wave to Carla, never mind her own pounding heart.

Peggy walked across the parking lot, unlocked her car door and slid in. Immediately, she pulled her iPhone out of her purse and texted Barb.

Manager ordered us out of gym. No surprise. It's a wrap. See you in car.

While she waited for Barb, Peggy pulled her laptop out from under the driver's seat and googled Edelweiss German Cuisine. Not a particularly imaginative name for a restaurant, she thought. And yet, after quickly scanning the first article, she discovered that Addison Weber was an artist turned chef, whose uniquely designed culinary presentations were making him into something of a local celebrity in the less than two years since he'd opened his business.

38

*B*arb yanked her vibrating phone off her waistband, and there was Peggy's text. She rushed out of the gym to her patiently waiting friend, anxious to relate her conversation with muscle man.

"There are good reasons to suspect all three men I spoke with today," announced Peggy before Barb could get out a word. "And with the priest already a suspect, that's four."

"Make that five," said Barb. "That weightlifter by the name of Joe."

"Joe too? How so?" A horn blasted behind Peggy when she didn't react after the traffic light turned green.

"Keep driving and I'll tell you. It was how he responded to one of my statements. I told him the police were focusing only on the few men who fit Tegan's exacting requirements. He said they'll be wasting their time when they get around to him. So how would he know he met every single one of her requirements?"

"She must have given him the eye."

"And if she did, maybe they made a date," ventured Barb. What happened with Milburn?"

Peggy paused, recalling the bad feelings she had while talking with him. He had narrowed his eyes and lowered his voice so that his tone was menacing. "That man has a mean streak."

"But Milburn's married."

"Tegan never told Becky a guy had to be single."

Peggy stopped at a traffic light and looked at Barb. "Then there are James and Addison to ponder. James was unnaturally quiet. Addison was worried to death. Maybe his anger had been building since Tegan broke up with him. At some point, she could have started hitting on him again. Then, three weeks ago, he snapped."

"But would Addison be the type to reduce her to complete helplessness and abandon her on the rocks?" Barb asked herself as much as Peggy.

"Barb, how would you feel about a sauerbraten dinner tomorrow night at Addison's restaurant?"

"I can taste the dumplings and sauerkraut now."

"Great. I'll call Cassie."

39

Peggy was about to sit down Tuesday morning with her usual breakfast of fresh blueberries, acid-reduced coffee, and oatmeal, to which she added two tablespoons of ground flaxseed and one tablespoon each of sesame seeds and sunflower seeds, when her cell phone rang.

A woman with a pleasant voice introduced herself as Samantha Winterly, the TV reporter who had spoken briefly with her at the crime scene on the Saturday before last.

"Ms. Crawford, someone tipped me off last night that you have been asking questions at the Sea & Shore Fitness Center. Can you and your two friends meet me and my crew this Thursday at the jetty for an interview?"

Peggy sucked in her breath. The three of them were now officially outed. "Let me check with the others. Do you know the name of the man who called?

"I'm sorry, I asked but he wouldn't say."

Peggy had figured correctly that a man had called. "Was there anything noteworthy about his voice?"

"Not really. He sounded very business-like, did not want to chat, quickly gave me the tip and hung up."

What will Mack think of my getting so involved with this? Peggy wondered. By this Thursday, it will be all over the news that I'm the one who found the body. Maybe it's a good thing he's out playing tennis with his buddies. He doesn't need to know right this minute.

At what time do you want us to show up?"

"By eight o'clock."

"Okay, Samantha, I'll call you back as soon as I know if Barb and Cassie can make it."

Peggy hurriedly got Barb and Cassie on the phone for a three-way conversation. "Samantha Winterly wants us to meet her for a live interview for *Good Morning San Diego* on Thursday. Can you be at the jetty by eight?"

After receiving affirmative answers, Peggy reminded her friends to keep their answers to Samantha's questions honest but also general enough so that the killer would not know their M.O. "We've only got till Thursday to gather clues without anyone recognizing our faces from TV."

"No pressure there!" snapped Barb.

"Cassie, I'll see you in a couple of hours. I only need a few minutes tops in Milburn's office to take pictures of those photos I didn't get to see yesterday."

40

"Okay, Chief, here's what we know so far." Thirty-four-year-old Sergeant Blane Sandingis sat down across from Police Chief John Bennett on that same Tuesday morning, then crossed one long leg at a 45 degree angle over the other to support his thick note binder.

"Tegan Hartwood was born and raised in Baltimore. Her parents were divorced early in her life and her father cannot be traced. She attended a small private college in Maryland, where she was a star runner on the track team. We have nothing so far on her whereabouts between the time she left college and six years later when her wealthy socialite mother died, leaving her only child her entire estate.

"Soon after that, Tegan's name started popping up in the press as the new owner of an art studio in the heart of La Jolla, as well as a successful artist in her own right. There were also a number of short features about her winning or placing among women in her age group in SoCal marathons or half marathons.

"After selling the studio 18 years later, at age 46, she moved to Carlsbad and concentrated on marketing her watercolor paintings to customers with plenty of change in their pockets. Painting in her own home studio, she continued to run her business and to exhibit her work in one of the La Jolla galleries until her death.

"As far as her connection with Sea & Shore Fitness goes, she started there part-time, two and a half years ago, as a Pilates instructor and personal trainer. Shortly afterward, she purchased her beach house.

"She lived alone, employed the same gardener as every other homeowner on her block, and used a top maid service as needed. She bought a new car each year. Didn't like to hold onto anything for long," Sandingis added wryly.

"All her background checks are clean."

Chief Bennett almost smirked. "She wasn't working at the fitness center because she needed the money."

"She was there for exactly the reason you think," said Sandingis.

"Her friend Becky Linley at the gym verified that Tegan sized up all the new men in her own classes, as well as those in Becky's. She also checked out the men who came in to work out on the machines or lift weights. Tegan enjoyed bragging about her sexy lifestyle but, on the other hand, she never named names."

"She wanted to keep her job," said Bennett.

Sandingis nodded, then continued. "We looked at her schedule book. All it shows for Friday, October 11, is *Dinner here, eight o'clock.*

"Out of the remaining men who met her specs, we dismissed those with rock solid alibis and those who were busy working out at the gym during the same time as Tegan's fatal dinner date.

"Tegan only worked three days of the week, so weekend warriors as well as men who never came to the gym before two o'clock were also eliminated. Tegan always left by two."

"So you think the murderer was a current lover?"

"Actually, Chief, the ME has informed me that she did not have sex recently."

"Dressed to the nines the way she was, she must have been salivating over a big date with a man who didn't want to have sex with her, but who visited her with the express purpose of poisoning her and then abandoning her on the jetty."

"Right. A man who hated her and whose methods were contrived to mean something significant to her."

"But wouldn't a woman sense that kind of hatred?"

"If the killer were an actor, he'd rate an academy award."

"So, Sandingis, where do you go from here?"

"I have directed my team to concentrate on the four most likely persons of interest we have so far— James Anderson, Addison Weber, Joe Markham, and Milburn Malawsky. There's also a Father Steven Caffrey but so far, he's on the back burner. Each of these men fits the general description given by our witness of a broad-shouldered man and each has the strength and intellect to have done it. None of them were working out at the gym or out of town that night. We need to dig deeper into each of their alibis."

"You're looking for an awfully big motive here."

"Dominguez, Wilkens, and I will be checking all of their alibis with a fine tooth comb starting this afternoon and continuing into tomorrow. I will check out Joe Markham's myself tonight."

"Any tip-offs from checking her iPhone and computer?"

"Dead end. She did not program her boyfriends' numbers into her phone, used it strictly for business. None of our suspects' names came up in texts or emails sent or received."

"No mushy phone chatter, nothing in writing. So how in hell did she make her dates?"

"Up close and personal."

"Okay, Sandingis, while I agree the odds are heavy it was someone connected with the gym, I would hope you'll stay open-minded."

Always am, Chief."

41

*L*ing dashed off a quick catchup story to the magazine editor about the latest official news on the murder case. However, some of the aspects unknown to the rest of the media would be saved for her final big feature article. She mentally reviewed her plan of action and then left after giving a big hug to Delphinium.

"I have plenty of helpful information to give Blane Sandingis," she said aloud, "but this is going to have to be a two-way street. When this case is closed, I expect him to give me an exclusive interview."

Delphinium cocked her head to one side as if trying to comprehend Ling's words.

Sandingis, fresh from his meeting with Chief John Bennett, was ready and waiting as soon as Ling was shown into his office. He stood, smiled as he shook her hand, then gestured to a seat that directly faced his desk.

"Good to see you again, Ms. Chen. When you called for an appointment, you mentioned that you have uncovered some information that could prove to be helpful in solving the Tegan Hartwood case?"

"Detective Sandingis, since the Saturday we first met at the crime scene, I've been working in close concert with the three women who discovered Tegan Hartwood's body on the jetty. So far, my stories for Seaside Magazine have been brief updates with only a few facts thrown in that the rest of the media weren't aware of. But what I am ultimately aiming toward is a lengthy, in-depth investigative feature story, fully loaded with side bars and photos."

Ling's straightforward introduction and openness had Sandingis' full attention.

"I came here today to update you and your team on our findings."

"Your reputation as a serious writer is well known, Ms. Chen. I'm anxious to hear what you've unearthed so far."

"I'll start with the revelation I personally have found the most disturbing. Would I be correct in assuming you are aware of Tegan's predilection for young, athletic, smart men and that therefore, you are taking a close look at several members of Sea & Shore Fitness, including a man by the name of Steven Caffrey?"

"Go on."

"I will take that as a *yes*. Do you also know that he is a Roman Catholic priest?"

Sandingis nodded.

"Well, last Saturday, I interviewed Father Steven at Saint Michael's rectory and uncovered something that could turn him into a prime suspect."

"Are you kidding?"

"Not at all, Detective. So am I correct that you kept him off your list of suspects because he told you he was a priest, and therefore you trusted that he couldn't possibly have been involved with Tegan?"

"We tend to dismiss priests and go with more likely persons of interest, at least in the beginning."

"And yet, they can be as complex and inconsistent as any other human being. Here is what you need to know. Tegan was a big donor to Saint Michael's summer drive for their parochial school."

Sandingis leaned forward in his chair and looked directly into Ling's eyes. "I don't like where this is going."

"After my interview, I went into the church and spotted two elderly women lighting candles in front of a Blessed Mother statue. I waited outside and greeted them as they left the building. They were all too happy to chat about the terrible fate of one of their fellow parishioners.

Ling's tone changed as she did a mock imitation. "Why, of course, they remembered Tegan Hartwood, and yes, she was so generous she even brought her donation of brand new educational toys and books to the rectory herself. The housekeeper, *what a fine upstanding woman,* found two large boxes of them one morning in early September, when she arrived at the rectory to tidy up and fix lunch for the two priests living there. The boxes were labeled, *From Tegan Hartwood, Toys & Books for Grades 1 & 2.*

Disbelief fought with curiosity on Sandingis' face. "Didn't everyone drop off their donations to the rectory?"

"Not at all. The church had requested all donations be brought to the storage room in back of the gymnasium during regular school hours."

Sandingis let out a long, low whistle. "Duly noted, Ms. Chen. Whom else do you suspect?"

I have to admit that initially I thought of an avenging moralist, someone who perhaps had killed other cougars."

"There are no unsolved cases that match the M.O. of this murderer."

"Could she be his first victim? Maybe her lifestyle, looks, attitude, or all of those put together, triggered repressed pain from an old wound."

"Possible. But for now, we're concentrating on the most probable."

"Someone like Milburn?"

"We got Milburn's prints last week at the gym, checked them in the database and came up empty. However, we did find a selfie Tegan had taken of Milburn and herself. Not on her iPhone. It had been transferred to one of her flash drives."

"Good. Let's add to that selfie the fact that Milburn and Tegan were alone together one night at the gym after closing time." Ling started speaking faster. "After that night, perhaps she threatened to expose their tryst to his wife. Something definitely went wrong between them because he and Tegan were not even on speaking terms when he gave her the Instructor of the Year award."

"It's a huge leap from not being on speaking terms with someone to setting up a date with them to commit murder."

"Could be she was making more and more demands—for money, promotions—including pressuring him into consenting to a full-fledged affair despite his marriage. He is young, met all of her criteria, and in her view, she might have considered him super exciting."

Following Ling's line of reasoning, Sandingis added, "So Milburn pretended to forgive her, accepted her dinner invitation, and started to put his diabolical plan into action? Doesn't seem to be enough of a motive for the extreme nature of this crime, Ms. Chen."

"She also could have had more dirt on him than their one-night stand, something from his past only she knew about."

"What else have you and your cohorts learned?"

"Addison Weber and Tegan were an item last December and up until March."

"That tidbit had gotten around."

"What if he initially had tried to get back into her good graces and was rebuffed? Then, what if, all of a sudden, she decided to give him another whirl and he finally accepted her invitation? Only this time, he was not about to be played again."

Sandingis' mood changed from curiosity and keen interest to one dominated by a feeling of protectivenesss. "Your information certainly is valuable to us, Ms. Chen, and I thank you for it. But I do have two concerns. We are used to tips coming in from residents of the communities in which crimes are committed and, at times, from non-residents. Naturally, I can understand Peggy Crawford's interest in this case.

"However, she and her two friends, with such a degree if immersion, have turned themselves into amateur sleuths. I don't know exactly how they have proceeded in obtaining these various clues but they could unwittingly have exposed themselves to danger. I am concerned about the safety of these three ladies." He paused and cleared his throat. "And of you."

Sandingis handed Ling a card with his direct phone number. "Promise to call me immediately, any time day or night, if you run into trouble.

"My second concern is that your final big feature story not be released until an arrest is made."

Ling's response was quick and firm. "I would never jeopardize your investigation. I can promise that my story will not run until the case is officially solved."

Her expression of deep concern told Sandingis all he wanted to know. As he looked into Ling's gentle, unguarded eyes, he smiled. "Somehow I knew from the first I could trust your judgment."

"I also have a couple of requests," she said.

"I owe you. Request away."

"Would it be all right for the four of us to see Tegan's house tomorrow? It will add color to my story to get inside and see how she lived."

"We've pretty much finished combing for evidence there by now. Wilkens will be reporting to the house at ten a.m. I'll tell him to let you and your friends in."

After thanking Sandingis, Ling had to ask, "I don't suppose you can tell me which men you are considering as suspects? Maybe they are the same as ours."

"Not at this point in the investigation. But I can say that with the addition of Father Steven Caffrey today, we are now concentrating on five persons of interest."

Ling wondered who, besides Milburn and Addison—whom he already had been seriously investigating, and now the priest—the other two suspects were. "How will you narrow down your list?"

"Any air-tight alibis would help."

Ling stood up. This time she was the one to extend her hand first. "I will, of course, notify you if we should come across anything else with the potential of being significant in finding the killer."

As Sandingis grasped her hand for a goodbye shake, his eyes held hers. "Now, what is your second request?"

Ling had to laugh. "Oh, I almost forgot. May I be the first to have an exclusive one-to-one interview after you make an arrest?"

Ling caught the almost imperceptible smile at the corners of his lips. "Even better. The minute I am ready to move in that direction, I will be in touch."

42

As soon as Ling left, Sandingis picked up his phone.

"Dominguez, we have a fifth person of interest. Go see Father Steven Caffrey at the rectory on the grounds of Saint Michael's Church. Tegan Hartwood brought boxes of toys and books for their school directly to the rectory one night back in early September. Apparently, the cleaning crew had finished for the day and the school doors were locked when she arrived.

"Ask him whether he was alone with her that night. Watch his reaction closely. Then inquire where he was on Friday night, October 11, between the hours of eight and eleven."

Dominguez was aghast. "To question a Catholic priest in this direct way... disrespectful, is it not?"

"In every case, there is a move the police hate to make. This is mine and yours."

"See him as soon as he is available today. And Dominguez, I expect you to use as strong a line of professional inquiry as you so capably do with anyone else."

"That priest is probably a saint," Dominguez murmured as he started out the door.

"In California, it's very challenging to be a saint."

"As far as I'm concerned, with the vow of chastity they take, all priests are saints."

43

James Anderson scoffed at Wilkens' question.

"Hate to mess up your gotcha intentions but I was in my office here till eight-thirty, much too late to carry out the elaborate machinations involved in the murder of Tegan Hartwood. I was working on some brand new ad copy, which I left on my secretary's desk for her to tackle first thing the next morning."

"Maybe you're a fast moving kind of guy. What'd you do after that?"

"Ever heard of Starbucks?"

As soon as Wilkens left, James grabbed his iPhone to leave a voicemail message for Addison. "Hey, I know you're at the restaurant and don't have time to talk, but I want to give you a heads up. A police detective was just here trying to break down my alibi. You must be next."

44

Addison was fully prepared to lay out an alibi when Wilkens stopped by his restaurant at two o'clock. His story was that he'd gone to a bash cocktail party in Rancho Santa Fe on Friday, October 11.

After getting the name and address of the host and hostess of the party, Wilkens took the obvious next step.

By two-thirty, he was pushing a button to announce his arrival for the hastily made appointment with the estate owners. The gate swung slowly open, revealing one of the most beautiful properties he'd ever been to. He already knew about the twelve bathrooms in the main house, walking path to the lavish guest house, which was bigger that the home he and his family lived in, extensive gardens, aviary, tennis courts, and indoor lap pool.

The head housekeeper greeted him politely and led him to a comfortable chair in the library and said that Mrs. Robinski would be right with him.

As she entered the library, he sized up the tall, super skinny brunette as forty-something.

"I can't imagine how I or my husband can be of any help regarding the jetty murder case, but I'm certainly willing to try," she stated as Wilkens rose to shake hands, then resumed his seat directly across from her.

"Mrs. Robinski, as a matter of standard procedure, we are checking the accuracy of alibis given to us by several of the men who belonged to the same gym where Tegan Hartwood worked. On the evening of Friday, October 11, Addison Weber said he attended a cocktail party here."

"Oh, of course, Addison was definitely here. Now there's a young man already on his way to the top in the restaurant business."

"Yes, ma'am. Do you recall seeing him here between eight and eleven?"

"Soon after the jazz singer and her band arrived, we enjoyed a few minutes of conversation outdoors on the patio."

"What time would that have been?"

"The musicians came on time—at seven-thirty."

"Did you see him after that?"

"With close to 200 guests circulating both inside and outside, I cannot say with absolute certainty that I saw him between eight and eleven. There was a lot going on that I had to direct—waiters replenishing trays of hors'doeuvres, the gourmet food spread and open bar—while trying to pay attention to each and every guest. Addison could have been anywhere.

"But I can say this. It was about eleven-thirty when some guests started leaving. He was among them."

"What about your husband's recollection?"

"Listen, detective, with the number of martinis he downed that night, I doubt he recalls anything. But I'll get hold of him right now on his car phone. His driver is taking him to Phoenix today for a conference. You can speak with him yourself."

"Before you do, I have one last quick question. How long ago did you *send* your invitations?"

"I always give four weeks' notice. Most of our friends and acquaintances have overloaded schedules and need to plan ahead."

Yeah, right, Wilkens thought, as he drove back to the police station. If the killer was Addison, he knew that party would provide him with an alibi hard to crack. So he set a dinner date with Tegan for that specific night.

"Could be, could be," he mumbled to himself.

45

"*G*ood evening. Have you ladies had a chance to look over the menu?" the rail-thin boyish looking waiter asked.

"We're all here for the sauerbraten dinner," said Peggy.

"With dumplings and sauerkraut?"

All three nodded.

"And for your drinks?"

"Two light beers on tap for my friends and herbal tea with honey for me."

"Easy enough. Thank you, ladies." As the waiter picked up her menu, Peggy caught his eye.

"Terrible news about Tegan Hartwood, isn't it? All of you must really miss her. Word has it she was in here frequently, up until right before her death."

"Tegan? Yeah, no, she hasn't been here for months. We often used to set up a table for Addison and her in the back office, and they would have dinner together there."

"Why did their get-togethers stop?" Peggy asked. "Did they have an argument?"

"Not the kind of argument with yelling and screaming. But I knew something was wrong between them because every time I entered Addison's office to serve another course, they'd both clam up real fast." The waiter turned to head toward the kitchen with their orders.

Addison had been circulating in both of the smaller adjoining dining areas. As he entered the main dining room, he spotted Peggy. "Well, well, well, we meet again. Is this for love of authentic German cuisine or for some other purpose?"

"A little of both," smiled Peggy. "My friends here and I are big fans of sauerbraten. I also was hoping to have a few minutes of your time, especially since you have a reputation for personally meeting and greeting all of your customers."

"Certainly. What can I do for you?" The restaurateur's smile was plastic.

"The day we met at the gym, you mentioned you used to date Tegan Hartwood but that you both had moved on. But I've got to wonder if Tegan had wanted a brand new beginning, would your old romance have been rekindled?"

"I'm not going there—it's not a real place."

"Though she was older than you and the other men she dated, she was still much too young to die."

"Like the food we purchase, we all have an expiration date." An insouciant double-dare-ya smirk accompanied his response.

"True enough, but having been close at one time, you must feel awful about the kind of suffering and death Tegan went through."

Addison adjusted his already perfectly centered tie and lowered his voice. "She most definitely had her faults. That aside, she never did anything specific I know of that could justify that kind of torture."

"Toying with others' emotions the way she did could have made at least one man decide enough was enough."

Addison's right hand grasped the knot of his tie again. Ignoring Peggy, he looked at Cassie and then straight at Barb. "I've got a lot of other tables to stop by. Enjoy your dinner, ladies."

As soon as Addison reached another table, apparently as far away from them as he could get, Barb spoke. "Definitely an uptight man about Tegan."

"He seemed calm enough about her death," added Cassie, turning toward Peggy, "until you zeroed in on how she was killed. Then he took your comment very personally and tried to totally exonerate himself as the perpetrator."

"Did you both notice that the pupils of his eyes were constricted?" Barb asked. "When conversations become too intense for someone, their pupils constrict."

A busboy was heading their way with three waters and a basket of oven-warmed bread. This time, Barb fired a question. "Your boss seems a bit on edge."

"Has been lately."

"I guess since his friend Tegan Hartwood was found dead?"

"Absolutely since then. We're all walking on glass around here."

"In spite of the major reason we came here," Peggy said as she got behind the driver's wheel, "I have to admit the meal itself, topped off with the peach and custard cream kuchen for dessert, was worth this trip."

"The elderberry dessert soup did it for me," said Barb.

"German chocolate cake and the art work," said Cassie. "Listen, on my way to the ladies room before desserts were served, I had to pass by one of the other dining rooms. Two huge paintings of panoramic ocean scenes caught my attention and I, of course, checked the artist's signature on each."

"Tegan's," Peggy said. She turned around before starting her car so she could speak directly to both of her friends. "So besides mutual physical attraction, Addison and she certainly had a lot in common—art, cuisine, and physical fitness—which would have taken their relationship to a more meaningful level than most. It must have hurt deeply when Tegan dropped him months ago."

"Had either he or she recently tried to renew their relationship?"

"Or…is he now so afraid primarily because his reputation and career would be smashed if he were publicly named as a suspect by the police?"

Peggy turned her key in the ignition, then hesitated. "And we also have to ask why James was so adamant that Addison and Tegan had no relationship whatsoever, when it must have been obvious to him that they definitely did."

46

Buddy Holtwater grabbed his cell phone from where he always kept it on the counter behind the bar and speed dialed the cab company. The dispatcher assured him a driver was nearby and would pull up in front of the Beach Scene Bar & Grill in less than five minutes.

This is the only part of my job I hate, thought the normally good-natured bartender. Seasoned as he was in dealing with the cross-section of humanity who stopped in to relax and have fun, it was the occasional falling-down-dead drunk, like this one, who never ceased to vex him. Why do they let themselves get to the point where they cannot function, especially if they are alone. Well, there was no way in good conscience he could allow this guy to drive himself home.

A few minutes later, Buddy walked his customer to the waiting cab, opened the back door and helped him get inside. Then he quickly returned, laid out some more chips and dip, refreshed drinks, and poured a couple of seconds. As his eyes swept the moderately occupied room rapidly, he realized it was only nine thirty. By ten thirty, the popular bar in the heart of Encinitas would be packed even though it was a Tuesday night.

A neatly dressed man Buddy had never seen before came in and stood at the far end of the bar, then pulled a black wallet from the inside pocket of his blazer.

"How can I help you?" the bartender asked.

"I am hoping you can tell me if you've ever seen this man," said Sandingis, opening his wallet to display his I.D., then holding up the photo in question.

"That's Joe Markham." Buddy smiled broadly. "He's a regular. Has been coming in most Friday nights for at least a year now."

"I need to know if he was in here the Friday before last, October 11."

"Yeah, he was. I remember because when he got here, he started talking real loud and laughing with some of the other regulars right away, before I even served him one drink."

Sandingis' eyebrows shot up. "And that was odd why?"

"Because he always arrives here cold sober and starts out real quiet, isolated, eyes straight ahead, not interested in anyone else. Like he's in his own world.

"Then, it only takes two Bloody Marys— he never has any more drinks than that— and the guy morphs into a 360-degree different personality."

"How so?"

"He gets off the barstool and circulates all around this horseshoe counter, cracking up my customers with jokes and entertaining them with friendly banter."

"Don't most of your customers get friendlier as the night goes on? Nothing unusual about alcohol-induced sociableness. Does he ever get drunk?"

"Hell, no, far from it. He basically changes from a loner to a sociable guy with personality plus."

"So you're saying on that particular Friday night, one week and a half ago, he was mister sociable from the moment he arrived?"

Buddy nodded.

"What did you make of his behavior? That he had already downed a couple of drinks at another bar?"

"If he did, that would have been a first."

"So did Joe order his usual two Bloody Marys after socializing for a while?"

"Not a one."

"You let him occupy a bar seat without spending any money?"

"He ordered a round of several kinds of snacks for everyone sitting at the bar as soon as he came in. He kept things hopping here and spent plenty of cash."

"Ahhh." Sandingis shifted his feet slightly so he was now standing at an angle which, he hoped, would make him appear less confrontational. "Now this is very important. Do you recall what time it was when he first came in the door?"

"It could have been pushing eleven. All I know is it was before eleven fifteen because that's when I take my break."

"I assume Joe always arrived alone."

"Yeah, and before you ask, I can tell you he always left alone."

Sandingis thanked Buddy Holtwater and headed back to his townhouse after an exhausting day. As he drove, he analyzed what he had learned. Joe Markham knew precisely how much alcohol he needed to release an ability to connect with others. So why the deviation from his customary pattern on that one night out of the entire year? Had he already swigged a couple? Was the answer as simple as that?

Joe's alibi is that he worked late and then drove to the Beach Scene Bar & Grill. He never mentioned going to any other bar. Of course, he could have had a drink either at his computer shop or home before going out.

Sandingis scratched his head. Even so, he thought, his alibi is not unshake-able. If Joe is the killer and he left the jetty by ten thirty, he could have made it to the bar in Encinitas well before eleven, in plenty of time for Buddy to have observed his raucous behavior before taking a work break.

Had Joe Markham purposely put on an act that night?

47

"If Milburn said he was home all night, why have you come here to question me?" Gloria Malawsky was clearly miffed about the interruption to her normal routine.

"Ma'am, it is standard procedure for the police to check all alibis." Wilkens had purposely set their appointment for Wednesday morning at eight thirty, when Milburn would not also be present. "We need to know if you are absolutely certain your husband was home during the entire evening of Friday, October 11. Is there any possibility that he could have left at any time without your knowing it?"

Gloria frowned as she reconsidered. "I went upstairs about seven to take a shower and relax. I work fifty hours a week. Friday and Saturday nights are my only time to enjoy diving into the pile of mags and books on my bedside table. So believe me, officer, I was very content not to be disturbed in the bedroom while he stayed downstairs to watch a football game he had recorded. When I came back down here sometime after eleven-thirty for a cup of warm milk, he was snoring in the recliner and some sci-fi movie was on."

"Thank you for your cooperation," said Wilkens as he showed himself out. Milburn and Gloria lead completely separate lives, he realized. They occupy the same house, that's all.

Alone once again, Gloria paced back and forth in her living room. If Milburn had gone out at some point, I would not have even known, she had to admit to herself. We don't pay any attention to each other after dinner and, truth be told, he's run around before.

48

"Father Steven, he's a wonderful priest…," Dominguez began. Both he and Wilkens were seated across from Sandingis in the lead detective's office for their scheduled three o'clock meeting Wednesday afternoon to discuss the five alibis.

"Skip the praise, Dominguez," said Sandingis. "Did he tell you where he was the night Tegan Hartwood was murdered?"

"In his room reading the Holy Scriptures."

"The entire time—from well before eight until eleven?"

"He fell asleep at his desk at some point, and the next thing he knew it was almost midnight. He shut the desk lamp and got into bed."

"Did the senior priest verify Steven's alibi?"

"He said they both said good night and retreated to their respective rooms by seven o'clock. He did not see or hear Steven leaving the rectory at any time."

"Let's move next to Addison Weber."

"Dominguez looked down at his notes. "Addison is the owner and head chef at Edelweiss German Cuisine in Oceanside. I spoke with his general manager who checked the schedule book and said one of the other chefs was cooking the night of the murder. He verified that his boss had gone to a party in the Ranch.

"I followed up with the estate owners in Rancho Santa Fe. Mrs. Robinski spoke with Addison at the beginning and at the end of their party, but not in between. Mr. Robinski, unfortunately, does not recall anything about their party except that the booze was flowing."

Sandingis directed his next question to Wilkens. "When you questioned Milburn's wife this morning, was she able to verify the alibi he gave us the first day we questioned him at the fitness center?"

"At first she said yes, he was home all night. But when I asked how she could be sure, she admitted she went up to their bedroom to read after dinner and did not come back downstairs until sometime after eleven-thirty to find him asleep in the recliner."

Sandingis shook his head. "Okay, let's keep moving. What happened with James' claim to have worked in his office late that Friday night on some brand new ad copy?"

"Sure enough," Wilkens responded, "James' secretary said she found the new ad copy waiting on her desk when she unlocked the agency's front door at eight the next morning."

Sandingis got up and began to pace. "So we know James created a new ad for his agency. Only trouble here is he could have prepped the ad way ahead of time, knowing he would need to be free in the weeks to come for a late meal with Tegan.

"Did any of the Starbucks employees recall seeing him after he finished working?"

"Too many people were coming and going, and apparently, he's not a regular there."

"I hate to say this," Sandingis stretched both of his arms out wide, "but none of the five men's alibis is 100 percent shatterproof.

"I grilled the bartender at Beach Scene Bar & Grill, who assured me that Joe Markham actually did show up the Friday night in question, only he could not swear to the exact time. He said the odd thing was Joe had a pattern of always arriving sober and somber but on that particular night, he arrived loud and rambunctious.

"Which leaves us with two possibilities. Joe had already downed a couple of drinks, maybe at some other bar, before driving to Beach Scene Bar & Grill, or he was purposely putting on a big show so we would think he had."

"And therefore could not have committed this murder," Dominguez completed Sandingis' sentence. "Because the killer would've had to be cold sober and clear-headed, not in the relaxed, fuzzy state alcohol induces."

"Or," offered Wilkens, "Joe could have arrived at Beach Scene Bar before eleven, super elated about having pulled off the most baffling murder case we've ever had here in Carlsbad. Maybe his true personality was released—no alcohol needed—after killing Tegan."

"No question he's a smart man," continued Wilkens. "He worked his way through college, then started his own computer business in his senior year with two employees who go out to customers' homes. The business is top notch with high earnings."

Dominguez looked frustrated. "We haven't been able to drop any of our five persons of interest."

Respected by the police department for his patience and persistence, Sandingis took a deep breath and then exhaled slowly. The meeting had been long enough. It was already four o'clock. Returning to his desk, he looked directly at his two detectives, then spoke in a calm, even tone. "We are missing a few pieces of this puzzle. Continue to keep digging. We'll put it together."

A few minutes later, Sandingis waited for one of the five possibles to answer his phone.

"Father Steven, this is Sergeant Sandingis."

"Detective, I don't know why you're calling. One of your detectives was here yesterday and I told him everything I can."

"Sorry to have to disturb you, Father. Look, I don't know what you and Ms. Hartwood did or did not do, but you were alone with her, which leads me to wonder if she was threatening to let that fact be known to the church."

"Are you saying you think I killed her?"

"We are pursuing several lines of inquiry."

"I cannot say any more than I already have."

"An overly ambitious young priest with a desire to climb to a much more powerful position in his church could have enough of a motive."

"I am not your man."

49

A young man from the next-door property was waving and hurrying toward Peggy's car as she parked behind Tegan's house. Barb and Cassie were with her and happily, they were about fifteen minutes early for their appointment to see the house.

"Good morning, ladies. I'm Ben Mitchell from next door. I saw you on TV last night explaining your wish to help solve the terrible murder of my neighbor Tegan Hartwood. I'd like to share what I know if it would be of any help."

Peggy and her friends got out of the car and stood facing him. "We'd certainly like to hear anything you can add," Barb piped up.

"I should start by explaining that I used to own Tegan's house, as well as the house I live in next door. About two and a half years ago, a friend with a real estate agency gave me a tip that some knockout gal was looking for a beach house to rent in Carlsbad. It was lucky timing since my current tenants had given me only two weeks' notice they were leaving.

"Anyway, I had been renting to her since then," he said, pointing to Tegan's house, "and what do you know, back in August, she made an offer to buy my rental property for more money than the already sky-high price it commanded because of its location. Said it was her dream home, perfect for painting the sea from the top floor sunroom, and also close to the gym, where she was working."

Ben was talking non-stop. "I was relieved. No more worry that she might get a whim to move out and I'd have to start renting it out again—a hassle. So I met her at the gym during her lunch break a few weeks ago to complete the necessary paperwork."

He paused to take a deep breath. "But here's what I want to tell you. The night she was murdered, lights were on in her kitchen, as well as in the dining and living rooms, when I happened to glance over there about nine o'clock. So I knew she had some guy there for dinner.

"When I went to bed at midnight, the living room lights were still glowing through her closed shutters but the other house lights were off. At the time, this struck me as odd because all the downstairs lights were always out before eleven when she entertained her boyfriends." He winked. "I got up at four forty-five in the morning to use the facilities and those living room lights were still on."

Ben stopped rambling and looked expectantly at Peggy.

"Did you also happen to notice what kind of car her dinner guest was driving that night?"

"Wish I had, but Tegan must have let him park inside her garage thinking he would be staying the night."

Barb was getting antsy. Looking at her watch, she said, "Well, thank you for the information, but we really have to get to our appointment to see the inside of Tegan's house." As she excused herself, she could not help scrutinizing Ben, a confident young man, full of vitality, overly anxious to talk about the murder. And someone apparently obsessed with watching Tegan's comings and goings. A voyeur?

"He didn't give us anything new," said Cassie, as they approached the front door. "A waste of time."

"In his effort to feel important," Barb added, "he let slip that he was at the gym a few weeks ago."

"Forget it, Barb," laughed Cassie. "He's not good looking enough to be a suspect."

"Agreed," said Peggy. "But how much would you like to bet that his friend with the real estate agency, the one who gave him the tip about a hot gal looking for a house, was James?"

50

"The forensic team has finished searching the house for evidence," Wilkens said, greeting Peggy, Barb, and Cassie. "You have a good forty-five minutes before I need to lock up and report back to the station."

Casual elegance would best describe the décor, Peggy thought, as they walked through the first level. She paused in the dining room. "I can't help picturing Tegan having her last meal right here at this table, unaware she was being poisoned."

Continuing into the living room, she added, "Afterward, they probably sat on that sofa talking until the poison immobilized her."

"The killer had to have very carefully carried her out and that's why he wasn't able to switch off the living room lights," said Barb.

"Come on," said Cassie, breaking their trances, "let's go upstairs to see what we're all dying to see."

Cassie was the first to enter the shoe room. "Look at all the blue shoes!" she exclaimed.

"They're not simply blue shoes," observed Barb, "they're many kinds of blue—royal, navy, baby, teal, azure, on and on. The range of colors and styles here is unbelievable." She spun around, taking in the hues of reds, yellows, purples, and greens.

Cassie picked up a pair. "Gladiator sandals—for when she felt or wanted to feel bold."

"Red, six-inch heels—a blend of femininity and power," said Peggy.

"And those effortless slingbacks on the top shelf—for when she was feeling playful, adventurous, ready for anything," said a familiar voice behind them.

Laughing, they all turned to greet Ling.

"Let's face it, shoes have been a form of self-expression for centuries. Tegan was an artist who admired and collected women's shoes, which have become a true form of art over the past few years," Ling commented, as she grasped the enormity of Tegan's shoe display.

"Don't you automatically check out other women's shoes?" Peggy asked, addressing her question to everyone. "What women wear tells you something about their mood. Jimmy Choo once said the right shoe can make everything different."

"Look at that section with colorful street-stylish sneakers," Ling said, pointing to the wall on their left. "Tegan's way of pairing high fashion with gym class footwear." A sandal that was a hybrid of sporty practicality with couture beading also caught her eye.

Realizing they only had 20 minutes left to see the rest of the house, Peggy suggested they concentrate most of their time in Tegan's bedroom, bathroom, and art studio.

Not the décor, in fact nothing in her bedroom was gender specific. Walls were painted pale taupe and the king-size, custom-made bedspread displayed cream colored seashells on a sand colored background. Several of her paintings graced the walls. "No girly-girly look to turn off the men," side-cracked Cassie.

While Barb, Cassie, and Ling chatted amicably in the bedroom, Peggy wandered into one of the most luxurious bathrooms any commercial showroom could ever boast.

The area of the counter for Tegan's makeup was tidy, with all of her beauty products in attractive containers. To the side of one of the sinks, a beige plastic container with two small round sections caught her attention. It was a case for contact lenses.

A few powder grains remained on the countertops. Knowing forensics already had dusted for fingerprints, Peggy felt no qualms about opening each side of the case. It was empty. She instinctively made a mental note that Tegan wore contacts and apparently had died with them on, although she wondered how in the world this fact could be of any importance.

Returning the case to its spot, Peggy joined her friends as they headed up the steps to Tegan's art studio. "I can't imagine a more perfect spot from which to paint the ocean, sky, and beach," she noted, gazing down at Tegan's work area, a long, wide counter with a double sink on one side, and then straight ahead through the window at the spectacular panorama.

The sunroom allowed plenty of space for up to four paintings in various stages of development to be laid out at the same time. A long desk in back of the room was flanked by file cabinets and faced several comfy chairs. This was where sales contracts were drawn up and signed. File drawers contained information on all of Tegan's customers, with whom she kept in touch by email to announce new art for their consideration. Not surprisingly, the storage closet was filled with canvases of all sizes, art magazines and supplies, and completed paintings.

After a few rounds of the three oohing and ahhing over Tegan's paintings and the view, Wilkens called from below the staircase that it was time for him to leave.

51

*T*he faster he ran across the loose sand of the dunes, the more the monster with its scaly, green rattlesnake head and tan coyote body gained on him. The sun scorched and shriveled his skin. Cacti needles spiked his legs. He screamed until his parched throat hurt so much he could emit no sound.

Distorted fragments of the repressed scene woke him like a shard of glass. He was wrapped in a film of perspiration and his breathing was rapid. Ever since he'd made his murderous decision, he'd had similar nightmares at sporadic intervals.

He thought the tortured dreams—a succession of images, each one overlaid by the next— would end once she was dead. But no. Those deep breathing exercises that the gym's trainers always swore by did nothing for the tension in his gut. He was still exhausted all the time, even though his schedule had returned to normal. *Samson felt his strength returning after his great sin, why don't I?*

After showering and dressing, the man went into the kitchen, opened the fridge and pulled out two extra-large brown eggs. After cracking the eggs and watching them slide into a plastic bowl, he picked at them repeatedly with a spoon, trying to remove the yucky white globs, those twisted rope-like cords attached to the ends of each yolk. Knowing that the purpose of the opaque spindled strands in the thick layer of egg whites is to anchor the yolks did nothing to stop his overwhelming feeling of utter repulsion.

While growing up, he'd always volunteered to prepare the eggs. *Why are people oblivious to the revolting chalazae? And eggs are in so many dishes. That's why I'm super vigilant about ingredients.*

As if this wasn't enough, he noticed a minuscule red speck in the bowl. This was even trickier to remove. He felt a wave of relief as he scraped it up along the side of the bowl and then flicked it off the spoon and down the sink drain.

Before sitting down to his omelet, toast, and cup of coffee, the man automatically clicked on the tiny TV kept on the counter. Samantha Winterly's voice on the morning news show was strong and clear. The omelet would have to wait.

52

"On this unseasonably warm morning for Thursday, October 24, I'm standing on top of the jetty at South Ponto Beach, where the body of Tegan Hartwood was discovered 12 days ago by these three women."

Turning to face Peggy, Samantha Winterly continued. "It must have been an enormous shock for you and your friends."

"Of course."

"Carlsbad police are investigating, and the lead detective on this murder case has assured the community that every effort is being expended to solve it. Our news editor received a tip that you also have been doing some sleuthing of your own. Why is that?"

Peggy looked straight at the camera. "I believe there's a reason the three of us were the ones to find the victim early that Saturday morning. We had a duty to report this cruel murder immediately, which we did, and we have a continuing responsibility to contribute our time and efforts in whatever ways we are able toward helping to find the perpetrator."

Barb was quick to back up Peggy's sentiments. "You don't casually walk away from such a shocking scene and go on as usual, as if nothing has happened. It's in our minds and guts every minute; we'll never forget it. Taking constructive action to help makes it possible to sleep at night."

"Are you getting any closer?"

"If and when we do, the police will be the first to know. Anything and everything we uncover, the police, and only the police, will know up until an arrest is made."

"Have you considered that the killer might perceive you as a threat?"

"A threat? Really? The kind of mind that could conceive and carry out such an intricately complex scheme might be afraid of three baby boomers who like to walk and talk along the beach? Threatened by us? No. Annoyed? Maybe."

The reporter wanted to also hear from Cassie. "Don't you believe the police are capable of solving this case?"

"Definitely. But this is not their only case, and with the economy, they have limited time and manpower. There are many little extras they cannot get to."

"The police always look to the community for any and all information that can help lead to justice," Peggy added. We mean to be one of their most supportive links."

"Thank you, ladies. From Carlsbad, this is Samantha Winterly."

53

Yanking the TV cord from its outlet, the killer went back to his bedroom where he pulled on a pair of disposable gloves and started printing a message on an unlined index card. Pleased with the end product, he placed the card inside an envelope.

Well, Ms. Peggy Crawford, maybe this will help you see the light, he thought. And once you do, I hope you will tell the police so they will spend less time and effort trying to find out who I am, and go full force after the real criminals in North Coast San Diego.

Reenergized, the man returned to the kitchen, ate his breakfast, and then started to prepare a special marinade for the salmon he would eat that night for dinner. Before pouring it over the fillet, he turned the salmon over and began to arduously scrape off its dark gray underside. When bears catch salmon, the only part they eat is this repugnant fatty layer so they'll gain weight before hibernating, he knew.

As he left ten minutes later, he was filled with a sense of relief that he could finally enjoy the fitness center without her piercing eyes following his movements.

54

By a little before ten o'clock, Cassie parked directly in front of Computer Haven, the business owned and run by Joe Markham, information supplied by Becky in response to Peggy's text.

Almost two weeks ago, Tegan had dinner with a killer. Am I about to meet him? she wondered as she pulled open the door to the shop.

"I'm looking for a new PC, something thin and lightweight."

"Really? And you coincidentally happened to pick my shop?"

Cassie ignored the sarcasm in Joe's voice. "I liked your ad."

"Cut the crap, lady. I don't know what your game is, but I'm not playing. I know you're one of the three broads trying to pin a murder on someone at the fitness center. One of you even had the nerve to question me while I was over there trying to work out."

"The opposite, actually. I'm trying to help along the process of elimination of suspects. The sooner we narrow it down to one or two, the better. Don't you agree?"

Joe Markham stared at her as if weighing the validity of her statement. "We got off to a bad start," offered Cassie. "Let's start fresh. Since you've been watching the news, you're familiar with the fact that the community is very upset about the cruel nature of this crime and wonders how a monster like the killer can stand to live with himself.

"Do you also know what's trending on Twitter and Facebook? That nothing can justify abandoning Tegan Hartwood to die in a totally helpless condition on that jetty."

Stoney silence.

"I only have a few quick questions, the same ones we're asking the others. How well did you know Tegan?"

"I was never one of her boyfriends and absolutely never wanted to be, not even for a nanosecond, if that's what you really want to know." The timbre of his voice was building.

"Where were you on Friday night, October 11?"

"Not with her. And yeah, I have a great alibi. When the police check it out, they will eliminate me and you simply will have bothered me for nothing."

"In that case, before I leave, is there anything at all you can think of that could help solve this case so Tegan can finally rest in peace?"

Joe played deaf. "Listen, my two employees are out on house calls. Now I really must get back to repairing these computers for my serious customers."

Peace is something earned, he thought, as he watched Cassie go out the door and press her car key fob.

Peggy was not picking up so Cassie spoke after the tone. "Peg, I want to give you a couple of my quick impressions from today's sleuthing.

"Hate to tell you but Milburn's not the only furious suspect. Joe Markham despised being questioned about Tegan, expressed zero remorse about the way she died, and the super odd thing is he never mentioned her name even once. He referred to Tegan only with pronouns. Let's ask Barb if he also avoided Tegan's name when she spoke with him at the gym."

Cassie snickered into her phone. "Joe might be a computer whiz, but my opinion is he does not have the ethical chip.

"As far as my takeaway from the art gallery, it's that Tegan never let anyone get in the way of her plan to live long and totally free.

"Until someone did."

55

*I*t was almost seven that night when the young librarian stationed at the first floor information desk returned to her computer after helping a patron locate a DVD. An envelope with Peggy Crawford's name printed across the front immediately caught her eye. She picked it up curiously, noting that it was sealed, then took two steps at a time up the staircase to the second level, where she knew Peggy would be working at the reference desk until their nine o'clock closing time.

"Did you see who left this?" Peggy asked.

"No, and I was only gone a minute. Whoever left this here must have been in an awful hurry."

After ordering a book from another library, Peggy stopped to open the envelope. The words were hand-printed in block letters.

LET THE DEAD BURY THEIR DEAD.

JUSTICE WAS DONE!

Peggy slipped the note back inside its envelope, told her coworker she needed to make an important call, took the elevator down to the first floor, and walked outside.

From the other end of the line, Barb's voice was emotional. "Peg, the killer knows who you are, where you work, and that you are sleuthing around. At the very least, he perceives you as an annoyance, but maybe Samantha Winterly was right that he might view you as a threat. She kept her word not to use our names during the TV interview since we didn't want them spread around to the general public, at least not yet. Even so, the writer of that note certainly has your personal information."

"Milburn already knew my name, and any of the other suspects at the gym could easily have gotten my name and where I work from Carla. But Barb, don't you see? If this note is from the killer, he has just handed us his motive—to enact justice for some terrible wrong that was done."

"Done to *him,* or to someone he cared about?"

"To him. 'Let the dead'—He is the one who is dead, dead in spirit. That quote is in the Bible, somewhere in Matthew."

"Are you going to tell Mack about the note?"

"When the time is right. I believe whoever sent the note is harassing me in hopes that we will give up our sleuthing. Somewhere along the line, we must have hit a nerve."

"Or else he wants to clear his conscience. Moral laws flow within all of us. Even those who do evil rationalize some justice in their act," Barb emphasized.

"All of which leaves us with one core question: What was Tegan's secret?"

56

Cassie was already waiting in front of her house when Peggy drove up. By eleven forty-five, they found the perfect parking space from which they could see, yet not be seen by Milburn. A few minutes before noon, they spotted him backing his car out from a reserved spot close to the fitness center's front entrance.

"Here we go," said Peggy, pulling back her hair, popping on her hat and sunglasses. "I'll only need a few minutes tops once I get inside Milburn's office. I know you have to tutor a high school student this afternoon, and I need to be at the library by two.

"At this time of day on a Friday, so many members are going in and out that Carla will be too distracted to notice me, especially with you entering the gym first and making a beeline for the front desk to engage her in conversation."

Cassie released her seat belt and opened the car door. "Sounds exciting. I'm with you all the way."

Carla looked up from the pile of papers she was sorting into the face of Cassie, a woman who was truly interested in finding out all she could about the center and what it had to offer. This was the part of her job Carla relished—meeting enthusiasts like this attractive woman, and she certainly elicited praise from Milburn every time she signed up a new member. If she nailed this prospect, she might succeed in helping Milburn out of the foul mood he'd been in lately.

Cassie immediately plunged into the attention-getting opening she had rehearsed in her mind. "I've heard so many good things about this gym. I'm in the middle of running errands right now, but I can come back tomorrow. Would I be able to try it out for a couple of days before I join?"

Carla's eyes danced as she quickly grabbed a free-trial signup sheet and plopped it in front of Cassie. "Yes, of course, we've got a great reputation for our amenities and wide range of classes. Let me tell you about some of them."

As the two women spoke, Peggy entered the gym in the midst of a group of members and headed straight down the hallway. She turned the knob to Milburn's office and quickly closed the door behind her. Exactly as Carla explained, the four photos from the framed collage had been disassembled and were in the back of the promo drawer. After laying the photos across Milburn's desk, Peggy pulled her iPhone from her pants pocket.

Snap, snap, snap, snap. There. Got them. I'll take a closer look later, she thought. Placing the photos back and closing the drawer, Peggy left as silently as she had entered. As she was headed back up the hallway, a man who was standing behind Cassie waiting to speak to Carla turned in Peggy's direction and stared into her eyes with an *I know what you just did* expression and a shake of his head. Would Carla also notice Peggy when she tried to slip by the front desk on her way toward the exit?

Unaware she had been holding her breath, Peggy exhaled long and loud as she left the building and walked to her car. As soon as she sat down, she texted Cassie as they had prearranged.

Reacting to the signal, Cassie smoothly extricated herself from the conversation with Carla, thanked her, and turned toward the door. She could hear Carla's friendly tone toward the man who had been waiting behind her.

"Oh, hi Steve. How's it going?"

"Who was that?"

"From my half glance I'd say it was Peggy Crawford. Milburn doesn't want her coming in here anymore."

"Well, how will he feel when he finds out she snuck into his private office?"

"Was she carrying anything out of it?"

"Nothing. Not even a purse."

Cassie walked away as slowly as she could but, upon reaching the door, had no choice but to exit. I wonder how Carla reacted to that last piece of news and if she'll decide to tell Milburn or not, she wondered.

When Cassie was only a few feet from the car, she was startled to see Peggy practically jump out of the driver's side to approach a man in a long-sleeved plaid shirt and khakis parked three spaces away.

"James, this is lucky timing," Peggy called out. "Remember me from the café last week? Do you have a minute?"

"I remember you but sorry, I'm on my way to work." His bland, opaque smile said, *Back off.*

"I will get directly to the point. Look, when we spoke, you emphasized that you only occasionally took Tegan Hartwood's classes. But she was also a trainer so you must have had some contact with her when you worked out on the machines. Were you ever involved with her?"

"That's none of your business."

"You do realize you are one of the men at this gym being checked out by the police. Someone as reticent to talk as you could become a prime suspect, and I'd be happy to give them you."

James' face curdled. "I can't believe this. Are you working for the police?"

"Let's say I'm doing some serious digging that may help. If you're not guilty, maybe you can deflect the spotlight from yourself by answering a different question. Did Tegan ever say anything at all that could throw some light on whom she dated that fateful Friday night?"

"The only morsel she tossed my way was that she'd decided to spend more of her time with super challenging minds, which would have been a pretty insulting comment if I had ever been one of her boyfriends. But no, Tegan thought of me as Addison's friend, nothing more."

"What do you know about Addison's past relationship with her? Could he have come back for more?"

James took a step back and crossed his arms.

"Addison and Tegan had art in common, sure. But I wouldn't dignify their time together with the word *relationship*. With her, it was about laughs and flesh on flesh. She wouldn't, maybe even couldn't, sustain a relationship."

An edge of bitterness to James' tone of voice plus his defensive body language did not escape Peggy's attention. He had also side-stepped her question about Addison coming back to Tegan.

Without another word, James got inside his car and started the engine. I don't have time or patience for snoops like this woman, he thought. I've got a couple of clients coming to my agency this afternoon who are looking for a house in the Ranch in the multimillion dollar range.

He could feel the old resentment building. Tegan—like a queen in her tower looking down at everyone on the beach—believed every single man in the world wanted her, and she could decide if and when someone would become her next boyfriend. She thought she could live like that forever.

Well, I'm the one who's still alive and kicking and she's not.

"The name of the guy who told on me was Steve?" Peggy asked in astonishment when she and Cassie finally settled back in the car. "Did he have a light complexion, sandy brown hair, and tower over everybody?"

"Poster boy for Irish good looks."

"He fits the description Ling gave me of Father Steven, the priest she interviewed last Saturday."

"You mean that priest is a member here?"

"That's what Ling found out."

Cassie grinned. "Well, no wonder he gave you a disapproving look for being so sneaky."

"Main mission accomplished; that's the important thing," said Peggy. "And besides getting shots of Tegan's photos, I was able to rile James up enough, right now in the parking lot, to unearth his long-held deep resentment toward Tegan Hartwood. A lingering resentment."

"While we're on the subject of James, you raved about the attention-getting loafers he wore last time you spoke with him. What kind of shoes did he have on this time?" Cassie teased.

A wide smile crossed Peggy's face. "Since you asked, today he was wearing Zanotti's crocodile embossed black leather high-top sneakers with side zippers."

"You've really gotten into shoes," Cassie chuckled.

"What can I say? I've got shoes on the brain. Tegan was an obsessive shoe collector and I wouldn't be at all surprised if James wasn't under her spell when he started purchasing incredibly pricey shoes."

"What do you think they went for?"

"Anywhere from fifteen hundred to two grand."

57

*B*arb readjusted her bra straps and let out a long exasperated sigh. "Too much time on a gravity sucking planet," she mumbled.

When she was director of nursing care in a large hospital, she used to advise the younger nurses, "People only care about how you make them feel, not that you're having a bad self-image day." Now it was time for her to put her own advice into practice.

Drew was not home yet so Barb settled in his recliner, put her feet up, and snapped on the TV for Friday's five o'clock local news.

"A Roman Catholic priest could possibly be a person of some interest in connection with the Ponto Beach murder case." Samantha Winterly sounded almost jubilant as she spoke.

"A reliable source at the Sea & Shore Fitness Center reported seeing one of the three women who found Tegan Hartwood's body working out in the weight section, next to a member who is a local parish priest. She appeared to be questioning him.

"In keeping with responsible journalism, we will not release the man's name unless, or until, an arrest is made by police."

"You call this lie responsible journalism!" Barb screamed at the TV. "I never met that priest; he wasn't even doing any weight lifting at the gym when I was there with Peggy!"

Grabbing her iPhone, Barb immediately rang Peggy. "Can you believe this? The source had to be Milburn."

Peggy's brows furrowed as she listened to her distraught friend. "Whoever phoned in this phony tip wants to cast suspicion on Father Steven and away

149

from himself. The reporter's so-called reliable source could have been any of our other suspects. All Samantha Winterly wants is a story and she doesn't care who tells her one.

"I guess she's no longer playing nice."

58

When Peggy said she needed a second opinion about James as a continuing suspect in the jetty case, Ling couldn't wait to stop by the realtor's office Saturday and catch him off guard. It was October 26, exactly two weeks since she'd first met Peggy and her friends at the crime scene.

Peggy was likely at the beach right now for her bi-monthly walk and talk with Barb and Cassie. She imagined them discussing every single fine point about the case so far. She would catch up with Peggy later.

As luck had it this Saturday morning, James was finishing up with an elderly couple by reassuring them of a quick sale at, or close to, their asking price. As soon as they left, he turned to Ling with the ubiquitous question, "How can I help you?"

Ling handed him her business card and introduced herself as a writer for North County Seaside Magazine. Although she'd not met him before now, there was no mistaking the powerfully built, handsome man with light brown hair for anyone else but the owner of North Coast Living Real Estate. He could have only recently come back from a photo shoot for the cover of a men's fashion magazine with his up-to-the-minute apparel and extravagantly priced Berluti's sneakers.

"I'm working on a human interest sidebar about Tegan Hartwood that will accompany the next installment in my series of features about the jetty murder case."

"Why come to me?"

"You, as well as a few other members and staffers at Sea & Shore Fitness may have gotten to know her well enough to help me add color to my portrayal of her."

"Okay, I'll bite," he said, leading the way to his office. After they both were seated, he continued. "Tegan used to show me pictures of shoes she had chosen for a date and ask what color, fabric, and pattern dress would go best with them. Guess she thought since I enjoy apparel myself and often stage homes worth millions, I have a sense of what goes with what."

"And *did* you choose the heels she wore for her last date?"

James' tone changed. "No, and I wasn't with her either when she wore those silver heels."

Ignoring his sarcasm, Ling quickly shifted her focus back to Tegan herself. "She must have been thrilled to be named Instructor of the Year."

"She gloried in it. So much so that she splashed photos of herself in the hallway—as a marathon runner and even one way back in college as a track team star. When I saw that yearbook picture, I thought…" he began, and then stopped short.

"Please go on," encouraged Ling.

"Off the record?"

"I won't be quoting you."

"Well, I wouldn't have given her a second glance back then. Plain Jane, arrogant expression." He paused, remembering. "She strutted around the gym like she was a natural born raging beauty. Not!

"You really want the unvarnished truth? She was an uber-selfish heiress who immersed herself in whatever brought her pleasure—sitting around in her high perch at the beach painting, gluttonously collecting shoes, and reducing men to whimpering puppets."

"Somehow your friend Addison must not have felt like her puppet. He claims to have moved on and found a new girlfriend soon after their breakup."

"Look, I'm not stupid. I figure you're going to share our little talk with that nosy library lady and maybe even with the police. Well, you can tell them all that Addison wanted to get back with Tegan and that I'm fed up with keeping his secret."

"If Tegan had wanted to be with you, would you have been charmed, especially if she had not been your buddy's girl?"

James pointed his index finger. "I would never have chosen a woman from old stock when there were, and still are, plenty of Gen Y gorgeous women around."

"Mr. Anderson, there is one more question I have to ask. Before I do, I want to thank you for being so frank. What was your gut reaction when you first heard how Tegan died?"

James tried to smile but his emotions froze the movement and distorted it into a partial grimace. He looked past Ling at the door.

"My next client will be here any minute."

As soon as Ling closed the door behind her, James slowly got up, his hands dropped down at his sides, and he began pacing back and forth.

A picture of Tegan standing achingly close to him flashed across his mind. She held onto his shoulder to steady herself while she removed one of her shoes to let him feel its texture. That was several months ago, but the picture was as clear as ever.

What did I think about how Tegan died? he asked himself. For whatever amount of time she remained alive on that jetty, she knew what it felt like to be discarded like flotsam.

In her car, Ling composed a text to Peggy.

Hit my stride. Important clues. First: James said Addison had confided he wanted to reconnect with Tegan. Second: My impression is James resented not ever having been chosen by Tegan. He felt scorned. Did he want to punish the woman who did not want him?

Ling tapped the screen of her iPhone and hit *Send.* Then she headed to her office at Seaside Magazine.

59

Something Tegan said about her upcoming date during her most recent, and final, hair appointment popped back up in Anita's mind over the weekend and kept pestering her. "It could be something or nothing," she mumbled as she tapped the numbers on her cell phone before starting work on Monday morning.

"North County Seaside Magazine, front desk."

"I'd like to speak with the writer who is handling the jetty murder case."

"That would be Ling. I'll connect you."

In less than a minute, a melodic voice with a light Taiwanese accent asked who the caller was and if she could be of any assistance,

After a quick introduction as the owner of Anita's Salon & Spa, Anita drew in her breath and started to talk. "I'm calling in reference to the jetty murder case you have been writing about. Tegan Hartwood was a favorite client of mine. I've remembered what she told me about the man she had a date with on the Friday night she died." She hesitated.

Ling sensed the hairdresser's embarrassment. "I'm glad you called, Anita, and would very much like to hear whatever it was."

"Tegan said she didn't know why, but for some mysterious reason, she sensed that this particular man could turn out to last much longer than she originally thought."

After thanking Anita for her tip and clicking off, Ling stared at the words she had jotted down as Tegan's hairdresser spoke.

What was it that Tegan sensed about her killer? All the suspects in this case are smart, handsome, and successful, Ling thought. Why did that man touch a deeper part of Tegan that even she herself did not comprehend?

If Anita's recollection is an accurate one, could Tegan's remark help us move at least one or two of our suspects to the back of the line? Ling wondered.

60

This time the note was left at one of the checkout stations on a long counter at the library on Monday afternoon. The man watched from behind a row of bookshelves until it was noticed and picked up by a librarian. Then he left as quickly and quietly as he had entered.

Several minutes later, as Peggy pulled it out of the envelope, she immediately recognized the hand-printed block letters.

STOP PLAYING DETECTIVE LIKE AN AGING NANCY DREW WITH YOUR 2 FRIENDS POKING AROUND INTO A LIFE STORY BEYOND THE IMAGINABLE.

"I'll be back in a few minutes," she told the other reference librarian as she hurried down the steps and out the front door. Unable to reach either Barb or Cassie, she tapped in Ling's number.

"This is the second warning you've received and it's obviously from the killer," Ling responded, after listening to the wording of the note. "Peggy, you have got to tell Mack. Detective Sandingis also needs to know, ASAP."

"I'm at work and I've already been away from my desk too long. I'll tell Mack when I get home tonight. Would you please call Sandingis?"

"I'm on it."

Sandingis could feel his adrenaline pumping. "Thanks for letting me know about these two notes, Ling. I need to clear a time to meet with Peggy by tomorrow afternoon. This second note tells me she must have found out about something significant that set off an alarm for the killer."

"Do you think she is in any danger?" Ling's grip on her phone involuntarily tightened.

"Unfortunately, the four of you could be." He paused. "Now I *really* can't let you out of my sight."

"Aren't you glad we're in this with you?"

"For many reasons, Ling, as long as you stay safe."

Ling felt wrapped up safely in the warmth of his voice.

61

Frank couldn't wait for Monday afternoons at the library. That was when he'd always check out a different book, which he could immediately plunge into, right out front in the comfy chair the snack bar owner kept ready and waiting next to his stand.

In fact, there were so many afternoons that the retired elderly gentleman showed up, the snack bar owner affectionately referred to him as "an institution."

Today, Frank shifted slightly in his chair, inhaled the fresh oceanside air, turned the page of a thick history book, then paused to look up for another enjoyable activity—people watching.

His attention was attracted by a tall, powerfully built man hurrying into the library. His lightweight windbreaker, hood up, hid the man's hair color, but not his malevolent expression.

Less than two minutes later, Frank watched, wide-eyed, as the man rushed back out, picking up his pace as he headed toward the parking lot. Now why would that young guy race out of the library like that? Why, he didn't even take the time to check out a book!

Frank had gotten a full face view, one he hoped to forget as he tried to resume reading. But how could anyone concentrate after locking eyes with unadulterated evil?

62

Peggy reached for the clock on her side of the bed to see what time it was. Two fifteen and I still can't get to sleep, she murmured softly enough so that Mack would not be disturbed. When I showed him those two notes last night, he was deeply worried, she thought.

All the clues Peggy and her friends had gathered so far rolled through her mind like a video in fast forward. She turned from one side to the other, trying to get comfortable, as she reviewed her earlier phone conversation with Sandingis. He told me there must be something I did or said that the killer either witnessed or found out about and considers a direct threat.

Yes! Peggy suddenly realized, as she bolted up into a sitting position. That time I snuck into Milburn's office while he was out for lunch.

But there's no way it can possibly be Milburn. He's too awkward. The monster we're looking for is a man who was sure of foot, had the perfect balance, controlled movements, and enormous strength to carry out his murder plan. Recalling how Milburn had angrily walked toward her when she was in his office, Peggy could almost hear his heavy, clunky footsteps. Milburn trips, fumbles and bumbles, she thought. He involuntarily opens and closes his right hand unless he's got something in it. No, he's not the killer. Not all athletic persons are necessarily graceful.

Wait! Father Steven saw me leaving Milburn's office and complained about it to Carla.

Then again, she chats with everyone so word probably got around the gym.

So maybe there was something in that office the killer did not want me to see. The photos from Tegan's collage that were in the bottom desk drawer? she asked herself. But why shouldn't I and everyone else in the world, for that matter, see them? Why on earth would anyone at the fitness center care about how Tegan looked when she was only 20 or about the fact that she enjoyed running?

As Peggy lay back down, she determined that as soon as she got up, her top priority would be to take a good, long look at those photos. *Slow-w-w-ly.* This Tuesday, she finally had enough time off. But first, she needed at least a few hours of sleep.

63

As before, the oversized sun was burning his skin, and he was filled with intense fear. Only this time, the monster with its scaly green rattlesnake head and coyote body was at the wheel of a car. As the snake-headed coyote drove off, the creature howled, then called out, "Stay here, Billy."

The man woke from his nightmare Tuesday morning with dry, racking heaves. He lay there a few minutes, involuntarily sinking back into the dream enough for his mind to remember more and more chunks of detail. When he was able to breathe normally, he reached for the remote on his end table and clicked on a TV cooking show to clear his mind.

Unbelievable, he thought. After touching everything in creation in that kitchen, the cook is starting to shape those meatballs with her bare hands. Why didn't she slip on some disposable gloves? What if a snagged fingernail shaving gets into the ground sirloin or worse, what if she has sweaty palms?

That's why I learned early to cook my own meals.

64

The sun came streaming through Peggy's breakfast nook Tuesday morning as she poured a second cup of coffee. Mack had left for tennis two hours ago, and this was her first chance to look closely at Tegan's photos with no interruptions. While she was snapping pictures of them last Friday in Milburn's office, she'd only given them a cursory look.

I want to see everything connected with Tegan's Instructor of the Year Award because it was at or around that particular time something triggered the killer to start his planning. The award in itself? No way, she thought. More likely, something connected with it. Like maybe these photos?

Now she pushed her coffee aside, slid her iPhone in front of her, and pulled up all four photos that had comprised Tegan's collage. The most recent one, the photo Milburn had sent to the local media, was a glam shot showing off Tegan's intense cobalt blue eyes, porcelain-like complexion, and lustrous copper blonde hair.

Curious to compare Tegan's most current look with her appearance as a young coed, she swept backward past the other photos and focused on the full color college yearbook shot of 20-year-old Tegan holding a large trophy. She looked harder at the photo. That fire engine red tee shirt with her voluptuous figure would certainly catch and hold any man's eye. But it was Tegan's face that Peggy was interested in.

The caption proclaimed her as a rising star in track and field. Expected were the dirty blonde hair, tons of freckles, and plain-Jane look that Milburn and Becky, even James, had referenced. It was true she *did* look like an entirely different person back then.

But there was something else.

Am I seeing correctly? Peggy asked herself. With her fingers, she carefully enlarged the picture on her screen. I've heard about this kind of remarkable anomaly but have never actually seen anyone with it.

Peggy got up and hurried to grab Mack's magnifying glass from the top of his desk in the study. Returning to the kitchen table, she peered through the glass at Tegan's face, focusing first on one eye and then on the other. There is no doubt about it, she thought, Tegan had heterochromia. Her right eye was blue while her left one was green.

Recalling the contact lens case she had seen in Tegan's bathroom, Peggy wondered when the victim had purchased her cobalt lenses and undertaken her fabulous makeover.

Tegan looked glamorous as ever in the two color photos she had bypassed. The caption under one that had appeared in a glossy SoCal magazine hailed her as a 29-year-old, new to La Jolla, and second place winner in her age category in a San Diego half marathon. In that photo, her eyes were cobalt. The other showed her as a proud finisher in the Big Sur Marathon at age 37.

This means Tegan had to have camouflaged her natural eye colors before she turned 29, Peggy realized with a jolt. Unable to sit still, she started pacing. Dear God, can what I'm thinking be possible?

Only one photo in the collage showed Tegan's natural look. That one and that one alone showed her rare eye anomaly. But the general public never saw that particular picture. Only the staff and members of the fitness center would have seen that long-ago yearbook picture, simply because it was included in her braggadocious wall display.

Suspicion about a connection between that photo and Tegan's murder started to take shape in Peggy's mind. An ugly, shockingly outrageous shape.

"Last night, I promised to keep Mack posted from now on," she thought, as she grabbed her phone. "By now, he's left the tennis court and is happily perusing the aisles at Home Depot for supplies for his next project."

Mack answered before the second ring. "How's the case going?"

"Everything's coalescing."

"Coalescing? Is that code? What does that mean?" He sounded exasperated.

"Mack, there's no need to worry."

"You, Barb, and Cassie are dangerously over involved."

"Oh, come on, Mack. With visits to a shoe department, beauty salon, art gallery, priest's rectory, fitness center, and Tegan's house with a police officer present?

"Look, my love, I think I'm onto something big. I'll call you later."

Even before clicking off, Peggy had decided to make a conference call to Barb and Cassie. Time for some serious brainstorming, she thought. But first *I need to put pen to paper and make a few calculations.*

65

"**D**id I hear you right?" Cassie asked.

"I'm looking at Tegan's eyes right now," Peggy confirmed. "In this early photo of her, one is green, the other is blue. I'm sending the photo to both of you now."

In a few moments, Cassie also found herself gazing intently at Tegan's eyes. "And you think this particular photo is connected to her murder how?"

"One of our suspects saw it and…"

"He recognized her!" Barb blurted out.

"Her eyes were a dead giveaway as to her shocking identity."

Barb picked up on Peggy's train of reasoning. "Which means one of them knew her when she was young, before she changed her hair color and makeup and started wearing contacts."

"You've got it," said Peggy. "And when she won second place in a half marathon at the age of 29, a full color magazine photo showed a cobalt-eyed Tegan."

Barb let out a long breath. The sense of something dark nudged her on. "So he knew her before she turned 29?"

"Exactly."

There was a long pause, almost as if time had been suspended.

Peggy broke the silence. "Whoever she was in relation to him, and whatever bad scene went down between them, that's what got her murdered."

Cassie was astounded. "But that's impossible. The oldest suspect, Milburn, recently turned 29 himself. Each and every one of the suspects would have been far too young to have known Tegan over two decades ago. They all would have been little kids."

Barb felt as if she would burst. "Peggy, are you thinking what I'm thinking?"

"If my hunch is correct, the killer was indeed a kid—Tegan's."

"What? Her killer could actually be her own son?" Cassie could not believe this was where their conversation had led the three of them. It was as if she'd been looking at a diamond and suddenly, the light shined upon it at an angle which revealed another facet. Peggy could hear the face Cassie was making on the other end of the phone

Peggy clarified. "Yes, a son separated from his mother at an early age. Listen, I worked out an age chart before this meeting of our minds. The earliest Tegan could have given birth was at the age of 21, since she clearly was not pregnant in that photo of her at 20.

"Now, in order to recall his mother's exact eye colors as well as her overall natural appearance so precisely, the killer would need to have been at least 3 years old, wouldn't you both agree?"

"Highly unlikely before that age," Barb agreed.

"Okay, I'm with you on that point," added Cassie.

"Good. So if she had him when she was 25, the killer would have been 3 by the time she was 28, which is the oldest she could have been when she dramatically changed her looks."

"Because by age 29, she was already sporting her new look," Barb threw in.

Peggy resumed. "Following my age chart backward, down the line, if she had him when she was 21, the killer would have been 7 by the time she was 28.

"Amazing, Peggy," said Barb. "You've got the time frame for the age at which she gave birth down to somewhere between 21 and 25. Knowing how many years older than her son she could have been, I'm certain you also calculated the killer's age range."

Peggy felt triumphant. "Couldn't be clearer. The killer is now between the ages of 24 and 28. Reading from my chart, if Tegan was 25 years older than he and she died at age 49, the killer is 24. And so on."

Barb was busily subtracting numbers on a yellow-lined pad of paper. She upped the speaker volume on her phone and laid it on her kitchen counter. "Uh-huh. If she was 24 years older than the killer, he is 25; if 23 years older, he's 26; if 22 years older, he's 27..."

Cassie caught on. "And if she was only 21 years older, he's 28."

"The big question is: What did Tegan do to make her son want to kill her?" Barb asked.

"And kill her in the specific way he chose?" Cassie wanted to know.

Peggy contemplated for several moments before continuing. "There must have been some terrible secret in Tegan's past, one between her and her son. What could that secret be?

"The article that accompanied the photo of her at 29 stated she was single and residing in La Jolla. So we do know that at some point before Tegan turned 29, he was never in her presence again until he joined the fitness center. And of course, it was not until he saw that photo in the hallway that he realized who she actually was."

"How ironical that the two of them would end up at the very same fitness center!" Cassie interjected.

"The shock of the sudden realization of who she was plus whatever painful, repressed memory it awoke in him must have caused a psychotic break." Barb remembered from her career as a nurse that deeply disturbed patients, given the right trigger, could go off the deep end and commit heinous crimes only to end up in prison or in a mental institution.

Barb continued her analysis. "What we also know is Tegan did not want any ties. She told her hairdresser she never let anything or anyone interfere with her lifestyle. So we can deduce that she decided at some point her son was standing in her way. The method in which she parted with him must have been so cruel, it scarred him. That wound was reopened when he recognized her."

Peggy jumped in. "She and Becky did a lot of girlfriend talk, yet Becky was led to believe Tegan had always been free as a bird, never had a husband or any children."

"Then what did she do with him? Who brought him up? Adoptive parents? Good foster care home?" Cassie's questions tumbled out. "Think about it. All of the suspects in this case are healthy, educated, super smart, and successful in their chosen fields. None of those men grew up on the street.

"Peggy, you've got to bring all this to Detective Sandingis ASAP. It's a solid enough scenario."

Barb's words were equally encouraging. "Your analysis makes all of our other theories fall away. This is a game changer."

When she saw that the caller was Peggy, Ling picked up her office phone on the first ring.

"Drop everything. I have been in touch with Detective Sandingis and he's waiting to see us. I've made a stunning discovery about Tegan that explains her relationship to the killer. And with your assistance, we might even be able to flush out his identity. I'll pick you up in front of your mag building in about ten minutes.

"I'll be ready and waiting."

66

lane Sandingis and Ling listened intently as Peggy explained, point by point, how she had reached the shocking conclusion that Tegan Hartwood's killer could be her own son.

Peggy then added a strong finish to her scenario. "Think about it. That early photo of Tegan was part of a collage posted in the hallway of the fitness center exactly three weeks before I discovered her body. That window of time, or close to it, would have been necessary for the elaborate preparations for her murder."

Sandingis was leaning forward in his desk chair, eyes fixed on Peggy the entire time she spoke, the range of his facial expressions running the gamut from skeptical to intrigued to amazed. Would-be detectives had been calling in with wild theories since news first got out about the body on the jetty. But Peggy had now presented him with a logical, well-thought-out, detailed theory that could very well be the case breaker he had been hoping for.

During the time he waited for Peggy and Ling to arrive, Sandingis had put in a quick call to the ME, Mike Attison. Why hadn't he been informed that Tegan Hartwood had heterochromia?

"My assistant performed the routine task of removing Tegan's contacts," Mike had explained. "He's not here at the moment for me to question, but I don't see how he could have missed seeing her anomaly. Nevertheless, he did not note it in his official report."

A careless mistake, Sandingis thought, but even if Tegan's anomaly had been noted, it would not have been a red flag for any reason. Especially since, when I had examined Tegan's file, there were no photos from the wall collage in there. Those photos were found much later by Peggy, not in Tegan's file, but shoved in the back of one of Milburn's bottom desk drawers. God bless this woman and her hunches!

Now, Sandingis looked for the second time at the photo in question which Peggy had texted before her arrival with Ling. He stood up behind his desk. He had made a decision.

"In order to move from theory to fact, I need proof." Sandingis shifted his gaze to Ling. "How would you feel about publicizing a search for the son of murder victim Tegan Hartwood?"

"Absolutely can do." Ling could not have hidden her enthusiasm if she'd tried. "*Seaside Magazine* has an online presence so I can post the yearbook photo, along with my story explaining Tegan's eye anomaly, tonight. The print magazine will be in our readers' hands by tomorrow morning."

Ling had to grin at her own sense of irony. "As an added bonus, social media and the TV networks will jump at the opportunity to do the good deed of helping locate an unknowing son, who otherwise would be deprived of his inheritance. Poor thing," she added with a touch of sarcasm. "Little will they know, they will be helping you to find the jetty case killer."

"Exactly the angle I have in mind." Sandingis smiled widely. "Sympathy for the son."

Then he added, "If someone comes forward verifying they knew Tegan and that she had a little boy, the most likely motive for her murder will at once be crystal clear."

Both Peggy and Ling looked expectantly at Sandingis.

"Considering that Tegan was *abandoned* on the jetty, I'd say she abandoned her son when he was too small to do anything about it. He obviously wanted her to experience the same kind of helplessness and fear.

"Ling, Peggy, there's another plus to publishing this photo and story. If the killer *is* Tegan's son, it will scare him enough that he might make a mistake."

"Can't wait to drop the bait," said Ling.

67

After reading every single word of the story about the nationwide search for murder victim Tegan Hartwood's son, believed to be in his 20's, Maria Sanchez stared again at the picture in *North County Seaside Magazine*. It was Wednesday evening after a satisfying dinner of Creamy Chicken Enchiladas, and she couldn't wait to read the next installment in Ling's series about the jetty case murder. It was on the first page after all the ads.

"This is the same woman all right," she said to her husband, who was immersed in the sports section of the local newspaper. "Listen to this: *Although there is no record of Ms. Hartwood ever having been married, police have reason to believe she may have given birth to a son more than 20 years ago. However, neither a son nor any other relative has come forward to stake a claim to her formidable estate.*

"*The most current photo of Ms. Hartwood, who was 49 at the time of her death, has already been widely publicized. By printing this much earlier photo of her as a college track star at age 20, it is our hope at Seaside Magazine that someone from her past will remember her as the mother of a little boy.*'

"She *did have* a son and if he is still alive, he deserves the chance to claim his inheritance." Maria proclaimed her realization in such a loud voice, her husband put down his newspaper with a start.

"How can you be so sure?"

"I was his nanny."

68

Thursday morning, the receptionist at *Seaside Magazine* hurried back to the front desk to answer the insistent ringing. Before she could state the full name of the magazine and ask how she could help, the caller's excited, high-pitched voice asked to speak immediately to the writer named Ling Chen.

Ling put down her iced latte and grabbed the phone on her desk. "Hello, this is Ling Chen. I understand you have something important to tell me."

"My name is Maria Sanchez. I have been following all of your stories about the jetty murder case. All along, I have had an uneasy feeling that the victim was familiar because of her artistic talent and athletic ability, as well as her unusual first name. But I did not recognize her face in the photo that was previously published.

"It was not until I saw how she used to look a long time ago that I knew for certain." Maria paused and Ling could hear her suck in a breath.

"Are you saying you recognize her now?"

"Yes, absolutely, without one doubt. And I want you to know that she did indeed have a son. You see, I was his nanny."

Ling's adrenaline rush was so strong she pushed back from her office chair, jumped up, and knocked over her latte. "Mrs. Sanchez, I need to talk with you in person as soon as convenient. Do you live close enough to come here to the magazine office?"

"I'm at the south end of Carmel Valley but I will be home all day today if you're able to come here."

Ling would have driven as far as necessary to meet. "More than able, Mrs. Sanchez. Would about an hour from now be okay?"

"Yes, my memories of those days with little Billy are like they happened yesterday. He deserves to be found and informed that his mother has passed away and left a fortune. Maybe his rightful inheritance can take away some of the sadness he suffered as a child."

With all the publicity about his mother's murder, unless he is living under a rock somewhere, he knows all about what she's left behind, thought Ling. And he's not about to come forward and claim one dollar.

After getting Maria's home address, she tapped Peggy's number on her phone.

69

*P*eggy was already standing in her driveway as Ling pulled up a few minutes before ten.

"Maria Sanchez made quick reference to sadness in the life of Tegan's son," Ling explained, as Peggy slid into her car and clicked the seatbelt. "She also called him Billy. None of our suspects is a Billy, Bill, or William."

"Names can be changed. What else?"

"She was his nanny only for a short time."

"Does she know I'm coming along?"

"I'm certain she won't mind. She seemed anxious to meet, said she had clear memories of the boy. Let's see if the details she fills in about his childhood and his relationship with his mother support the motive Blane Sandingis put forward."

"Not only the motive, but also who the killer is. Once we know how many years ago Maria took care of Tegan's son and how old he was then, we will have our killer," Peggy said as much to herself as to Ling.

The next 55 minutes went by quickly with Ling talking in snippets, concentrating more on the eternally heavy traffic, a given in SoCal, no matter the day of the week or the hour. This Thursday, however, was Halloween, and Ling found herself tapping the break even while driving uphill. Peggy, meanwhile, was quietly mired in her own preparation of questions to ask the person who once knew Billy intimately.

70

"How can I forget the strangest job I ever had?" Maria Sanchez was ready and eager to recount the time she had spent taking care of Tegan's son over two decades ago. Peggy and Ling were comfortably seated on the couch across from her as she spoke.

"I was in between permanent jobs when I saw an ad for a temp nanny to care for one small boy during the summer. I figured that would tide me over financially while I continued to search for another long-term position. Over the phone, Tegan said their regular nanny had left, and she would be moving soon to a bigger house in La Jolla. Meanwhile, she needed someone to keep her son occupied during the day.

"She asked that I address her as Ms. Tegan and said her son's name was Billy. I was never given a last name and she always paid me in cash."

"How old was Billy?" Ling asked.

"That was another strange thing. Any proper nanny would naturally want to know the age of a child under her care. Not only did Tegan never tell me, but the one time I asked, she glared at me and walked out of the room."

Ling gently pressed the question. "Based on your experience as a professional nanny, how old did you estimate Billy to be at the time?"

For a second, Maria flashed back on Billy. "I can almost see him. He could have been as young as 4 or even as old as 6. The variations among young children in height and speaking ability are tremendous as you must know."

"And you cared for Billy how many years ago?"

"Right after Tegan and Billy moved, I was hired by a wonderful couple as a nanny for their two children. I was with them for three years until I got married and started having my own children. So that's easy to recall. It was 21 years ago."

Peggy shifted to the edge of the couch. "Mrs. Sanchez, can you share some of your memories about Billy?"

Maria grew sad as she flashed back and visualized Billy as a little boy. "He was quiet and smart, very smart. Brownish hair, cute, skinny. The only time the poor little guy could get out of the house was when I would take him for a walk or to the playground. No other child was ever allowed to come over."

Knowing Billy was between 4 and 6 when he was abandoned is huge, Peggy thought. This narrows the killer's age range down to 25 to 27. I had already eliminated Milburn because of his awkwardness plus his age. And now, Addison Weber, with his auburn hair and ruddy complexion plus his age, is free and clear.

Peggy was quick to ask another key question. "What was his relationship to his mother like?"

"Tegan would be out for hours and when she did come home, it was heartbreaking to witness the child running to his mother with open arms only to be rebuffed. She would go to her bedroom to paint or make phone calls and was not to be disturbed."

"Mrs. Sanchez, I will of course relay all of your information to Detective Sandingis before running my next story," Ling explained. "Your verification that Tegan Hartwood definitely had a son, along with his approximate age during the time you were his nanny, will go a long way in helping to locate him."

Maria cleared her throat and looked at Ling. "Whoever killed Tegan in such a cruel way is the devil incarnate."

Neither Ling nor Peggy was about to tell the trusting and good-hearted nanny that Billy was the killer. She would find out soon enough.

71

No sooner had Ling dropped Peggy off in time for her afternoon library shift than she called Detective Sandingis' direct number from her car phone. His line was busy.

She kept her message on his voice mail short. "Are you ready for this? The best person imaginable not only recognized Tegan in the photo we printed, but she is 100 percent certain Tegan was the mother of a little boy. She was his nanny! I'm driving directly to your office from just having interviewed the nanny in her home."

As Ling pulled into the police headquarters parking lot, Blane Sandingis waved from the building's front entrance. "Outstanding work, Ling," he beamed, gently supporting Ling's arm as the two of them quickly walked back to his office. "Tell me every single detail, leave nothing out."

"Not one of the nanny's words will be missed. With her permission, I recorded the entire interview, which was conducted by both Peggy and me. The nanny felt sorry for Tegan's son and said she is hoping her information will help in the search since, from her point of view, he deserves his rightful inheritance. She obviously has no clue whatsoever that when we find the son, we will have identified Tegan's killer."

Ling pulled her chair up close to Sandingis' desk, laid down her mini recorder and pushed *Play*.

As the recorder clicked off, Ling could not help feeling a sense of pride in what she and Peggy had accomplished. "Ground-breaking info, wouldn't you agree, Detective?"

The delight in Sandingis' smile reached his eyes. "Maria Sanchez's account is a massive break and I want to move forward ASAP based on what we now know, thanks to the continuing efforts of your friends and you.

"We begin by now definitely eliminating two persons of interest, leaving us with James, Father Steven, and Joe, who are within the age range of 25 to 27."

"I don't want it to be the priest," Ling sighed. "Yet he's the one who resembles Tegan the most—her natural look: light skin color, viridian eyes that are a mixture of her two eye colors, and even a sprinkling of freckles."

"Yes, but the identity and appearance of the killer's father are unknown. The perp could have looked like him, not Tegan."

Ling frowned. "His father either never knew Tegan was pregnant or, if he did, cared zero for the child."

"That college photo of Tegan has gone supernova, accruing thousands of hits on social media. So by now, the killer knows there is a nationwide search for him," Sandingis said.

"Before you write your next story, I'd like to see how each suspect reacts to the fact that this nanny has come forward with information about the young boy she once cared for, as well as about the relationship between mother and son."

The detective paused. "Ling, once again, I need special help here."

"Ready, willing, and able."

"Since you've been covering the jetty case from the beginning, it would seem only natural for you to be the one to give our persons of interest a call and catch them completely off guard, unprepared with scripted answers.

"Here's the plan. When you call them, go ahead and state that Tegan's son is estimated to be between 25 and 27. Now, the next thing you can tell them is for their ears only. It is important that, for now, you do not yet include this in your story. Say that when you inquired, police would not deny that they believe her son is actually one of their current persons of interest."

Sandingis jotted down the phone numbers for James, Father Steven, and Joe, and slid the paper across his desk to Ling. "I would prefer fingering the killer before the media and the general public get this specific information and pressure becomes so intense that the killer hires a lawyer."

"I can call the three men today, Detective, "and I will be anxious to hear your analysis of their gut reactions."

Sandingis' eyes twinkled. "I was thinking we could do the analysis together."

72

"Please, Ms. Chen, for the sake of the reputation of Saint Michael's Church, as well as mine, your suspicion that I may have committed the mortal sin of murder must be put to rest."

As Ling pressed her phone against her ear, Father Steven Caffrey continued to react to her statement. "You have told me that Tegan Hartwood's missing son might be one of the current suspects in the crime against her.

"First of all, you must realize that, as a Roman Catholic priest, there are things I'm not at liberty to talk about." He locked his hands behind his head and paused.

"What I can say is this: As humans, we can start to drift, but drifting is always downstream. If we see this happening and we ask God's help, He will always put us back on the right course."

"Thank you, Father. Neither the police nor I will be releasing the names of any suspects at any time. Only the name of the killer will be publicized at the time of arrest."

"Then I truly have nothing at all to fear."

As the call from Ling disconnected, Father Steven was thankful that he had not held Tegan Hartwood in unforgiveness in his heart. That would have only served to keep him in bondage, not her.

James Anderson interrupted Ling as soon as she told him about the nanny coming forward.

"What? You mean the son's nanny doesn't know exactly how old he was when she took care of him?"

"No, but you fall into the age range."

"What else have you got?"

"When I asked, police did not deny that finding Tegan Hartwood's son would be the same as finding her killer."

James' anger was vehement. "You cross-filed and indexed me the moment you looked at me.

"If it weren't so disgusting, it would be hilariously absurd that you think Tegan could in any way have been my mother. Listen and listen good. My mother always was, is, and always will be Martha Anne Anderson.

"If you want to waste more of your time, go have a look at the hundreds of photos of my mom and me from the time I was born onward. I'm sure she will be happy to show them off."

James hung up before Ling could say another word.

My final call. This should be satisfying, thought Ling, as she tapped in the number for Computer Haven. After explaining who she was and the reason for her call, she sat back in her office chair and waited."

The explosion came. "Why would you want to give *me* of all people a heads-up about such a far-out notion?"

"I am notifying all suspects."

"*Braaah. Vo.*" Joe Markham yelled into the phone. "What kind of reporter are you? There's no way I'm a suspect. Don't you know I was at Beach Scene

Bar & Grill when that over-rated Pilates instructor was killed? I was never near her that night."

Click.

73

*I*t was almost five o'clock Thursday afternoon when the killer broke connection from the worst phone call of his entire life. *That full of herself magazine writer shocked the hell out of me,* he thought, *saying that dead bitch's son is 25 to 27 years old and could be one of the current suspects in the jetty murder case. Said she wanted to give me a heads-up before publishing her next story. Yeah, right. What she wanted to do was scare me so I'd inadvertently reveal my identity by blurting out something incriminating.*

Hah! I completely snowed her. Let one of the others freeze up and say something stupid. That will get the limelight off me.

The killer dropped his face into his hands. *I can't believe things have gotten so far in the short time since the media announced the nationwide search for that woman's son. My nanny remembered her from that photo* Seaside Magazine *and the copy-cat publications ran. Worse yet, she also remembered me.*

It's all the fault of that nosey Peggy Crawford, the one who found the body and went on TV with her two friends to tell the world she planned to provide all the help she could to the police. They did a lot of poking around the gym, asking questions. But she was the one who found out about the Instructor of the Year photo display from one of the big mouths there. When I heard about her sneaking out of Milburn's office, I figured she'd found that photo.

Peggy, my dear, you've been much too clever for your own good.

He recalled in detail the moment of his epiphany, almost six weeks ago now, as he had stared at her photo in the gym's hallway, the one of her way back before she colored her hair and covered the natural color of her eyes with tinted contact lenses.

"Billy, I'm Billy," he had murmured. But no one had been there to hear him.

He looked at his watch. In a couple of hours, he would check to see if he could pull up Ling Chen's breaking news online. Until then, he had to appear like a man with nothing more on his mind than the work before him.

74

Sandingis listened to Ling's verbatim account of the suspects' reactions. "Knowing the writer you are, I'm certain you also jotted down your own impressions of each of the three men," he said. "I wouldn't be at all surprised if they are the same as mine."

Anxious to share her conclusions, Ling had called the detective immediately after speaking with the suspects. "I'll start with Father Steven," she said in a jubilant tone. "From his response, I could extrapolate he'd had one intimate encounter with Tegan with no follow-ups."

"Same," Sandingis smiled into the phone.

"And personally, I cannot help but be relieved and delighted," Ling added. "Now for James. He volunteered who his mother is. Easy to check out."

"Right. It's not James."

"Joe had the 'how dare I call him' attitude. When he said he's not a suspect, I thought, *not a suspect anymore*."

"Exactly. Not a suspect—the killer."

"You know what they say, Detective, great minds think alike."

"Isn't it time you felt comfortable calling me Blane?"

"Blane, it is. At least, when no one else is around."

"Like during this phone conversation."

"So, Blane, what's next?"

"Go ahead ASAP with your story per our agreement about what to leave out for now."

"And for you?"

"We know Joe Markham is both Tegan Hartwood's son and her killer. My job now is to gather enough evidence to show he had a huge motive—revenge for abandonment, a most cruel abandonment."

"I'll hear from you when you are ready to make the arrest?"

"Sooner than that, Ling."

As soon as Sandingis hung up, he picked up his desk phone and punched out some numbers.

"San Diego County Child Protective Services," the robotic voice announced. "If you know the extension of the person you want to reach, enter it now."

The lead homicide detective knew exactly who could and would put other work aside to search county records for placement of an unidentified, abandoned 4-year-old boy 21 years ago.

75

At eight o'clock Friday morning, the first day of November, the killer booted his computer, then pulled up *Seaside Magazine's* website and searched Jetty Case Murder. There were several stories going back to the day the body was discovered. He clicked on the most recent one, published only minutes ago, headlined NANNY REVEALS JETTY MURDER VICTIM HAD SON, and read it.

With all the publicity, Tegan Hartwood's son would have to be living on a remote island not to know by now that his mother is deceased and he is eligible to inherit her formidable estate. Why hasn't he come forward? For what possible reason could he be keeping his identity secret?

How can this be happening? he wondered. He could feel his body start to heat up and perspire. His mind was spinning with Ling Chen's insinuations and conjectures.

Her questions will get people thinking all sorts of things. But at least she didn't publish her suspicion that the missing son is also one of the men suspected of murdering her. Why did she hold that back? Maybe she lied, and she's the only person who put that together, not the police.

What should I do now?

After pacing back and forth for several minutes, he hastily showered, dressed, and drove to work, skipping breakfast. He reviewed the day's work orders with his two employees and then went back to his personal computer to check if Ling's story had been picked up yet by the rest of the media. Hell, yes! It had rippled through time and distance. Each headline smashed into his gut like a punch from a heavy-weight boxing champ.

WHERE IS TEGAN HARTWOOD'S SON NOW?
TEGAN'S SON WAS SAD CHILD, NANNY SAYS
WHEREABOUTS OF SON UNKNOWN FOR
MORE THAN 20 YEARS
TEGAN AND YOUNG SON WERE SEPARATED—WHY?

He closed his laptop. No use reading the list of stories in the other publi-cations that have an online presence. Too many.

Instead, he turned on the TV. Switching from channel to channel, he whizzed by the flurry of news reports about the discovery of the nanny. Then came the worst one: "*Who raised Tegan's son?*" a reporter asked.

No, no, no, no. Are they going to find out where I grew up and the reason I came to be in that place? That would provide police with my motive.

He inhaled deeply, held his breath a few seconds, and then exhaled as slowly as possible. But they could not prove opportunity. I was at the bar in Encinitas with witnesses galore the night of the murder.

The bar. How he wished he were there right now, where drinks, boisterous chatter, laughs, and small talk flowed and made him feel a part of something. Where they recognized him but demanded nothing from him. And they all thought, if they thought about him at all, that he hadn't a care in the world.

What I've got to do now, he knew, is continue to remain outwardly cool, and keep up my routine of work, the gym, and other regular activities.

76

When Peggy got home at six that night from the library, there were live reports about the nanny all over network and cable news. It would be front-page news throughout California by tomorrow, and many of those following the breaking details soon would be inundating radio talk show hosts with calls. Reporters everywhere were looking for the most sensational angle and some had contacted Maria Sanchez to dig up more dirt. They don't know the half of it, thought Peggy.

Clicking off the TV, she succumbed to the irresistible aroma wafting from the kitchen and sidled up to Mack who was happily engaged in preparing his latest favorite dish: rotini with homemade tomato sauce. The pasta was already boiling and chopped, vine-ripened tomatoes were simmering in light olive oil. "Now see," he said, speaking as if she had been beside him all along, "the pasta sauce people pick up in grocery stores can't compete with this." Peggy watched as he added a sprig of fresh basil, a pinch of dried rosemary, a few shakes of dried oregano, and two quick dashes of sea salt to the pan. "A few more minutes and my masterpiece will be ready."

"How much longer will police hold back the identity of Tegan's son?" Mack finally asked Peggy after they'd both enjoyed their first few bites of rotini.

"They won't release who he is until they can actually arrest him.'

"What more do they need?"

"Proof of a compelling motive for murder."

"You mean like revenge for her abandonment of him? That does not seem enough of a motive for rendering her helpless against natural forces for hours before she finally succumbed. Sadly, there are many unwanted children who

190

end up in foster care or adoptive homes. But they don't grow up, find their bio mothers, and weave intricate plans to murder them."

"That's the piece of the puzzle that is missing—precisely what did Tegan do to rid herself of the child she never wanted."

"Must have been pretty nasty." Mack grimaced.

"The killer's first note to me said justice was done. The second note said I was poking into a life story beyond my wildest imagination. For some time now, I've believed Tegan must have abandoned him in a place where he would suffer greatly and then die."

"Except he lived."

"And was brought up by a person or persons who provided for his health and education," Peggy said, turning up the volume on the remote control. "This reporter's well known. Let's listen."

"Once upon a time, more than two decades ago, Maria Sanchez was the nanny for a little boy who apparently has disappeared from the face of the earth. According to Mrs. Sanchez, this boy was the son of murder victim Tegan Hartwood, whose case continues to be investigated since her body was discovered Saturday, October 12, on a jetty in Carlsbad, California."

Peggy switched channels, catching another report already in progress.

"Although the nanny was never told the boy's age, she estimated he was between 4 and 6 when she cared for him 21 years ago. Assuming he is alive, his current age is between 25 and 27.

"Tegan Hartwood was a wealthy woman—what with her inheritance from her multi-millionaire mother, earnings as a sensationally popular artist in SoCal, plus a beach house with a sunroom full of not-yet-sold paintings worth many thousands. Besides all this, the value of her amazing shoe collection to an avid collector is incalculable."

Peggy checked cable news.

"The mystery surrounding the jetty case murder has deepened as questions mount about the victim's son, whose former nanny has come forward after recognizing Tegan

Hartwood from a photo published in a local magazine. Those who knew her well at Sea and Shore Fitness Center say the 49-year-old Pilates instructor had a lifestyle unburdened by any children. In all published interviews of her as an artist or as a marathon runner, she never mentioned a child.

"A spokesperson from one of the La Jolla galleries, where her paintings have been displayed for two decades, said Tegan Hartwood was a free soul, who bragged she had ties to no one.

"The obvious conclusion here is that this mother neither wanted nor kept her son."

Then the reporter popped the hard questions in everyone's minds.

"So what happened to him? Was he abandoned? If so, where did Tegan Hartwood leave him? Was he found and given a home?

"Perhaps the truth will never be known. But if you are out there, Billy, claim your fortune and do some good with it. There are plenty of people who will be cheering for you, whatever has happened in your life and wherever you are."

77

The next morning, the phone calls started in a rush.

Blane Sandingis was not at all surprised when members of the press expressed indignation that they'd been scooped by Ling Chen. Their questions were always the same.

Why was *she* the one to get the nanny story first? Why didn't he call a press conference and inform all of them at the same time about the existence of a nanny who could confirm that Tegan Hartwood had a son?

And Sandingis' answer was always the same.

"It was the nanny's choice to get in touch with Ling Chen of *Seaside Magazine* first, in lieu of the police or any other media outlet."

Sandingis strode out of his office to the police station's front desk. "Any more calls from the press today must go to Wilkens. I'm waiting for an important return call from Child Protective Services. Please put it through to me immediately, even if I'm busy talking with someone else at the time."

78

Sandingis involuntarily raised his shoulders in high tension mode when the call finally was put through at ten thirty.

"The background on this kid is a gripper," said the familiar voice on the other end of the line. It was Paul Everett, a San Diego CPS supervisor whom Sandingis contacted in cases where a criminal he was investigating had been abused, neglected, or abandoned as a child.

"Turns out a Good Samaritan, exploring one of the many off-road, sandy driving trails in Anza-Borrego Desert, spotted the boy wandering about in a dazed condition. The boy did not know his name, age, or address, and appeared to be in shock. So he helped him into his pickup truck and drove him to the sheriff's office in Borrego Springs.

"At that time, there were no missing child reports anywhere in SoCal, although the boy appeared to have been lost in the desert for well over 24 hours."

No surprise there, thought Sandingis. Tegan did not want anyone searching for him.

Paul Everett continued. "That's when CPS stepped in to help. The boy was thoroughly checked out by a doctor, who confirmed amnesia, apparently brought on by shock. The doc treated his badly sunburned skin, cuts and bruises. The boy's age was estimated to be four."

"Exactly what we figured," said Sandingis."

"You should also know police departments throughout California were notified but no one ever came forward to identify the boy."

Sandingis could feel excitement building in his chest. "Where did CPS place him?"

"With no possible way to find out whom he belonged to, CPS placed him in a foster home near Borrego Springs that had a long-standing reputation for providing consistent quality care for children it took under its wings."

Remembering to breathe, Sandingis asked, "Is the home still in business?"

"It was run by Angela and David Holloway, who retired a couple of years ago. The good news is they're still living at the same address."

"I can't thank you enough, Paul. I owe you big time," Sandingis said, after jotting down the pertinent information.

"How about dinner at George's in La Jolla for my wife and me?"

"Great. After I make the arrest. And I'll be bringing along a friend."

Paul chuckled. "She's only a friend?"

"We'll see."

Clicking off, Sandingis' thoughts went straight to Ling. At five four, she was perfectly proportioned. Rich chocolate brown eyes a man could fall into. No heavy makeup or glitter necessary to cover her flawless skin and natural beauty.

Sandingis got up and grabbed his sun hat. My next interview will fit together all the parts of the most sensational murder case ever to hit the beaches of SoCal, he thought. The major reason he had chosen the profession of homicide detective was for the satisfaction and fulfillment in finding the truth, no matter how tangled a case may be.

He buzzed Wilkens. "Put on plenty of SPF. We're heading out to the desert."

79

The microwave oven beeped three times and Ling removed her eggplant parmigiana. Then she filled Delphinium's bowl with her favorite dog chow and placed it on the floor directly across from where she was about to sit at the kitchen table. The two of them enjoyed eating dinner at the same time whenever Ling was home.

"I wonder how much closer Blane is to arresting Joe Markham?" Ling asked out loud. Delphinium's ears perked up. Her friendly spirit and gentle, sensitive nature, Ling thought, surely made her the very best pet imaginable.

"I've been preoccupied day and night about this case for three weeks now. Tomorrow, I'll take you for a good long run and give you some extra attention," she promised.

At that very moment, the phone rang.

She knew his voice right away, a voice any radio or TV newscaster would kill to have. "Ling, I'm sorry to call you this late, but I just got back from the desert. Since we spoke the other day, the complete story about Joe Markham's background has come together. I thought you'd want to know sooner rather than later."

"You were so right to call. I can't wait to hear why you were way out in the desert."

"Turns out that Tegan Hartwood abandoned her son there. If not for the kindness of a stranger, who found the boy and took him to the local sheriff's headquarters, Joe definitely would have died."

"How could she have been so cruel?"

"Child abandonment with every reason to believe your child will die, and wanting that end result, is attempted murder."

"He lived, but she accomplished the murder of his spirit."

Sandingis took in Ling's compassionate analysis. Crimes were not simply black and white to her. Someone had been deeply hurt and could bear it no longer. But no matter what, murder was never the answer.

"Child Protective Services placed him with foster parents, who were well-regarded in the area. They cared for him until he left for college."

Could the unknown part of the story have been there all along? Ling wondered. Her excitement was building rapidly. "You questioned Joe's foster parents today?"

"They recognized Joe the instant I showed them his photo, although they have not seen or heard from him since he was 17," Sandingis elaborated. "They had named him Joe Smithson so they were a bit surprised he had changed his last name.

"Over the years together, no matter how much they tried to connect, he remained emotionally detached from them and the other children in the home. He never did recall who he was, where he was from, or what had happened to him."

"Until he saw Tegan's college photo." Ling paused while arranging her thoughts. "Did they have any information about his education?"

"Yes, he won a scholarship to Cal State. He told them his work as a teacher's assistant in the computer lab would take care of any additional money he needed."

"You're wrapping up the case?"

"I'm so close I can taste it. But there is one more thing I need to do to put the case over the top. Before making any arrest, I always make certain I have gathered every possible shred of evidence."

"You are extremely thorough, Blane."

"As are you with your feature stories."

80

It was almost four o'clock the following morning when he finally gave up on the possibility of getting any sleep. As soon as he rolled over to his side and let his feet hit the floor, he headed straight to the closet.

He could feel his hands start to shake as he pulled the navy blue wool blanket from the zippered bag, unfolded it, then spread it out on his bed. Bending down over it, he inhaled her scent, still strong inside of the blanket he had wrapped around her on that fateful night. He remembered she smelled the same way on the day he had stood close to her as they made their date and also on the Friday night he'd sat next to her on the sofa. But how would her body smell by now? Putrefied and revolting.

After inhaling deeply a few more times, he refolded the blanket, put it into the bag, and returned it to the closet. He should throw it out. But no, not yet. Not quite yet.

The old dialogue in his head from long, long ago started playing. The first voice said, *"You must stay here, Billy. I am leaving."* The second screamed, *"Mommy, mommy, no, don't leave me here. I want to be with you."* Then she answered, *"But I don't want you. Arrivederci, mi amore."*

The scene shifted suddenly in his mind.

He was completely alone in the desert wilderness, running, running as fast as he could, screaming at the top of his lungs, thorny cacti digging into his calves, something sharp gashing his leg. At dusk, collapsing against some huge rocks. And then it started. The series of short, falsetto yips that strung together, then blossomed into quavering howls that resembled maniacal laughter. All night long, the barks, yelps, and growls, woofs, and high frequency whines as the desert coyotes communicated with each other.

She heartlessly abandoned me to a host of possible endings, he knew, each of which would have been horrific—snarling coyotes with their arched backs and lowered tails tearing his flesh, the scorching desert heat draining his body of any trace of fluid, starvation, snakebites, insect or scorpion bites.

A hard reality became clear.

No wonder I always suffered a throbbing loneliness, an interminable searching for something nebulous. No sense of belonging, of worthiness, of confidence.

At least I had the satisfaction of telling her she had ruined my life. When I left her on the jetty, the final thing I said was, "You killed me long ago, now it's your turn to die."

He sat ramrod straight and pressed against the cane-back chair.

Self-defense is considered justification for killing in any court. I was too little to defend myself back then. What I did was not murder.

It was self-defense delayed!

81

By three thirty Sunday afternoon, the sun was strong so Peggy walked straight to the table with the largest umbrella in the Starbucks courtyard.

Immediately after Ling told her about the latest giant leap forward in the case, Peggy had relayed the news to her friends and arranged a meeting for the four of them. The case they had worked so hard on for the last three weeks was about to come to a successful conclusion, and each of them arrived within the next few minutes with a heightened sense of anticipation.

Ling's smile could not have been wider as she plunged right in. "The answers to Joe Markham's mysterious background were at the foster home the entire time.

"But Blane Sandingis told me he has one more aspect of the case to check out before he makes the arrest. As soon as that takes place, he promised me an exclusive interview. Then, at last, I'll be able to release my full and final feature story.

"Cassie, thanks to the photos you took of Tegan's shoe on top of the jetty and of her body cradled in the rocks, I will be able to publish images no one else in the media was ever able to capture."

"Exclusive, private interview, huh?" Cassie teased.

Ling blushed. "Come on, Cassie, he'll be answering lingering questions like what was his first impression of Joe when he went to the gym two days after we found her body. Another thing none of us ever knew was Joe's alibi and why it didn't stand up.

"And what I really can't wait to find out about is what more Blane has to do before arresting Joe. He now knows for a fact that Joe had the motive, means, and opportunity to commit the crime. What else is he after?"

The question hung in the air for a minute.

"Well, friends, I've got to say I got a bad vibe from Joe the day I met him at the fitness center while he was lifting weights." Barb did not mind bragging a bit.

Cassie agreed. "He was arrogant when I questioned him at Computer Haven. It struck me as peculiar that he never once said Tegan's name."

"Me too," said Barb. "He only referred to Tegan as she, her, or that woman."

"Or that Pilates instructor," remembered Ling.

"All of that was distancing language." Barb knew.

Ling flashed back to her interview with Father Steven. "I'm happy it's not the priest."

"And not James. He seemed so downtrodden." Peggy could see him in her mind's eye.

Ling looked at Peggy. "Thanks to your theory that someone must have recognized Tegan from her early photo, we've gotten this far."

"In his first note," Peggy responded, "the killer let me know he believed justice was accomplished by abandoning Tegan to the forces of nature. That triggered the question I asked myself every single day after that. In what way, and when, had she done something similar to him?"

"Without the photo, I wonder if he would have eventually remembered that Tegan was his mother. Probably not," Cassie answered herself.

Barb could not wait to share her thoughts. "That's something we'll never know for certain. But the repressed memory of his traumatic separation from his mother could have started to surface eventually, stimulated by something seemingly innocuous, innocent—like a facial expression, an incidental touch between them at the fitness center, the pitch, tone, or rhythm of her voice, even a vaguely familiar smell. We automatically breathe in and decipher smells without being aware of doing so. Odor communicates between people.

"Nothing is ever lost from memory. When we say we cannot recall, it's only that we cannot retrieve the file—it's still in there. The memory of every single thing we ever did or said, smelled, touched, was said or done to us—good, bad, or indifferent—is still in each and every cell of our body. We simply are not conscious of it all.

"I should have trusted my gut feelings about Joe. Our brains pick up imperceptible things we don't consciously register and put them all together."

"So Joe's deep hurt from childhood explains his lack of self-esteem and detachment from others," added Ling.

Barb summed up. "The yearning for our mothers is inherent, no matter what. Joe was enraged, but I have no doubt he was also grief-stricken and lonely for a relationship that never was but should have been."

"And what about Tegan?" Peggy asked. "She sensed something special about Joe. For the short time that she knew him, could she have yearned for a long lasting relationship, not ever dreaming he was her son?"

Ling piped up first. "She lived a hedonistic life on the coast where the hot younger men surfed, kayaked, and worked out. As long as she had someone or was in the process of conquering someone, she was content. That was her fix."

"What were her thoughts as she lay dying on the jetty? That's something else we'll never know," Barb said.

Peggy raised her cup of hazelnut Macchiato. "Each of us has gathered different pieces of the same puzzle that ended up fitting together to compliment and support the work of the police. That's what we set out to do and we achieved it."

"Here, here," the four of them, clicking their coffee cups, cried out in unison.

As a leopard might stealthily survey a group of gazelles, hidden and from a distance, Joe watched the women from the shelter of a nearby shop. His eyes squeezed down to slits as he narrowed his choice to one.

She would be next.

82

As Wilkens parked the police car in front of Joe Markham's townhouse Monday morning, November 4, he could not help stating the obvious. "A guy like this is extremely dangerous. Rage doesn't switch off because he got his revenge."

"He's probably at Computer Haven by now," Sandingis said, looking at his watch. Either way, our search warrant came through this morning and we're going in."

Assuring themselves Joe Markham was not inside, Wilkens pushed in the front door. After a cursory look at the living and dining rooms the two men focused on the kitchen, making quick work of opening and checking the contents of every cabinet.

"It's what you thought, Sarge," Wilkens said. "Six of everything, nothing missing."

"Joe was too clever to use one of his own bowls for the poisoned salad. He bought a brand new bowl, knowing he'd have to leave it at Tegan Hartwood's house, that he'd need two free hands to carry her out.

"But I had to be absolutely sure," Sandingis added. "What I really came here for is most likely upstairs. If I find what I'm looking for, there will be no need for a DNA maternity test to determine the biological mother-child relationship."

Sandingis bounded up two steps at a time with Wilkens right behind. In less than one minute he had the layout nailed—two bedrooms, two bathrooms, one small office. He was primarily interested in the linen closet. Carefully, he removed a tiny plastic bag from the inside pocket of his blazer and held it up to the light streaming in from the adjacent larger bathroom.

"Now, Wilkens," he said, "let's see if we can find the navy blue wool blanket that matches this fiber Mike Attison found at the crime scene."

Wilkens pulled everything out of the top two shelves while Sandingis knelt on the floor and removed towels from the bottom shelf. Nothing.

Wilkens read Sandingis' mind, walked into the master bedroom and opened the closet.

Above pants, shirts and jackets on wood hangers was a wall-to-wall shelf filled mostly with books. To the far left was a four-inch thick zippered bag.

Wilkens pulled it down, turned, and handed it to Sandingis, who'd come up behind him. Neither said a word as the lead detective unzipped the bag and pulled out a navy blue blanket. He gently placed the fiber on top of the blanket.

"It's a match!"

"Congrats, Sarge. Your hunch that the killer might have kept it sure paid off."

Sandingis walked over to the queen size bed and spread open the blanket. How ironic, he thought. Joe Markham could not let go of the one thing left that connected him to the mother who had never wanted or loved him. Her scent.

"Bag it and meet me in the car," he told Wilkens. "This is going to be Markham's shortest, and last, day at Computer Haven."

83

At ten thirty that same Monday morning, Peggy stood still on the wet sand and watched for a few minutes as white caps rhythmically rose higher than usual and crashed violently against the jetty rocks. The sky was a canopy of stratus clouds. Mist blurred the horizon line. A few feet behind her a red flag waved next to the warning sign: DANGER, RECURRENT RIP TIDES.

She pulled her hat down on her forehead as a blast of wind threatened to take it out to sea. After a short, brisk walk, she planned to head home, eat breakfast with Mack, and then change into appropriate attire for the library. She made a quarter turn to the south, and started to walk. The stretch of beach ahead was all but deserted except for a man and woman walking in the distance. Only a few seagulls flew overhead.

A long, high wave crashed, spreading dozens of white lace, intricately patterned tablecloths across the shallow water. Tiny Speckled Godwits with their long bills and incredibly fast legs knew exactly when to scamper forward and backward, instantly responding to the various wave strengths.

It was two days ago when Ling said Joe Markham's arrest was imminent. What was holding it up? Unclipping her phone from the waistband of her black spandex pants, she tapped in Ling's number.

"Sorry to interrupt you at work, Ling, but curiosity can be both a blessing and a curse."

"Oh, hi Peggy. Where are you? I'm hearing static."

"I've started walking from the jetty toward Moonlight Beach."

"My story is written, polished and ready to go as soon as Blane notifies me he's arrested Joe Markham. I'm a cat on a hot tin roof."

Peggy knew the signal to her phone would be blocked as soon as she reached the bluffs along the coast so she stopped short of reaching them. As she was about to ask Ling to keep her tuned into any news about the arrest, she glanced to her left and froze.

A tall, broad-shouldered man with deep brown hair was running toward her at breakneck speed.

"My God, it's Joe!"

"What? He's there?"

The next thing Ling heard was Peggy's scream.

84

Sandingis and Wilkens parked in an empty space directly in front of Computer Haven and walked in.

"How can I help you?" asked an employee busy working on a customer's computer.

Sandingis pulled out his wallet and showed his ID. "We are here to see Joe Markham."

The employee stopped working. "Sorry, he hasn't come in yet."

"After ten thirty in the morning and he's not here yet?" Sandingis pointed toward the back room and Wilkens went to check.

"Strangely enough, no. He's always here early, never misses a day."

"So where could he be? Does he make house calls for sick computers?"

"No, never, he holds down the fort here and another employee and I do all the house calls."

"As soon as he either gets in touch with you or comes in…" Sandingis began, then paused as his phone rang. The screen showed Ling was trying to reach him.

She sounded hysterical. "Blane, Joe's got Peggy!"

85

Joe Markham grabbed Peggy's phone and threw it into the ocean. Before she could run, he got hold of one of her arms and started pulling her toward the parking area.

"Let's do this quietly," he said. "See, no guns, no knives. As you know, I am not a violent man.

"Here's what's going to happen. You and I will get into my car and I will offer you a drink, which you will accept. It will contain a most merciful poison and you will die quickly. No waiting and worrying like that other woman." His voice was low but his face was hard.

Peggy knew Ling would call the police. But could she buy enough time until they arrived?

They were walking rapidly and soon they would reach his car.

"Look, the police know every single thing about you. Hurting me won't stop your getting arrested for murder and going to prison."

"If I'm going there anyway, I might as well go with the satisfaction of getting even with you."

"But with a second murder, you would be hurting your own chances of ever being paroled."

They reached his car. Joe opened the passenger side door and shoved Peggy in. The thermos was on the dashboard.

"I feel sorry about what happened to you as a child, really I do."

"Hah! Bullshit! I sent you notes. I told you justice was done, that the circumstances were beyond your imagination. You rejected my pleas and you kept on digging."

He reached for the thermos and gave it a shake.

"At the time I received your notes, I didn't know your full story. What your mother did to you was horrendous."

"What kind of woman decides her child has no right to live? Entirely because I was inconvenient? She left me with a broken spirit, unable to forge a connection with any other human being." His voice cracked slightly and the anguish slipped through.

He started to twist open the thermos top, which doubled as a cup.

"I have to give you credit for moving forward with your life, studying and working hard to become such a successful businessman."

Her tactic was not working. Once he poured the drink, he would be able to easily overpower her and force her to swallow. She had to delay him. *God, please save me.*

His eyes were lasers. "It's all because of you that I'm going to prison."

"Joe, you would have been caught anyway. The police had you down as a suspect from the very beginning."

He paused with the thermos in one hand, cup in the other.

"There were other suspects."

"And I know for a fact that even without me, the police would have eliminated all the others for one reason or another."

"Without that photo, no one else would've ever hypothesized the dead woman was my mother."

"Not hypothesized. But," she paused, "they would have started looking into the backgrounds of each of you, asking who your parents were. They would have pieced it all together."

He started to carefully pour the drink.

"Joe, please tell me, now that your mother is dead, is your pain gone?"

He winced. "No, it's back, even worse. Her *put downs* keep playing in my head: 'You slow me down; You're a pest; I wish you had never been born; I should have been smart enough to abort you.'"

The cup was full.

Did she hear a siren? Yes, and it was getting louder. *I've got to try to reason with him one more time or it will be too late for them to save me.*

"So you felt relief at first but it didn't last? Joe, it would be the same if you kill me now. Hurting me won't change the wrongs done to you. Please, please, don't do this."

She closed her eyes and willed herself to pass out before having to drink.

In that moment, the police vehicle screeched to a stop beside Joe's car. The next thing Peggy saw was Sandingis smashing the driver's side window and pointing a gun at Joe's face. She could feel the poisonous contents of the thermos and cup spill all over her lap as the killer suddenly dropped them.

As Wilkens ran to the passenger side to assist Peggy, she said a silent prayer. *Thank you, dear God, thank you with all my heart.*

86

*L*ing grabbed her phone the split second it rang.

"We were able to save Peggy in time!"

The best news of all, delivered in Blane Sandingis' assured tone, was like balm to Ling's jangled nerves.

"Thanks to your immediate call, she's at home now taking it easy with her husband."

"What a relief! And Markham's in jail?"

"He's being held for the murder of Tegan Hartwood and for the attempted murder of Peggy Conti Crawford. I arrested him at the beach precisely when he was about to force her to drink poison."

Sandingis paused. "Ling, I promised you an exclusive interview as soon as the killer was arrested. If you can come by the station now, I'll be happy to answer any questions. I think you'll also be interested in what I found at Markham's townhouse this morning."

"I'll be right over."

"Great. My press conference is not until two o'clock so we'll have plenty of time."

Ling couldn't wait. Immediately after the interview, she planned to release the biggest feature story of her career so far. She would relate details her readers were waiting for as well as include two of the photos Cassie had quickly shot while waiting for police to arrive at the crime scene: one of the shoe that had dropped on top of the jetty, the other of Tegan's body sprawled across the rocks.

Cassie would be identified as the photographer since police do not release crime scene photos to any of the media.

Photos Ling herself had taken of Tegan's shoe collection room and of her sunroom filled with spectacular seaside paintings would also be run.

The story would break big and national, and she savored the knowing.

There was no need for Ling to stay for Sandingis's press conference after she finished interviewing him. Armed with all the details of the jetty murder case, she had a jump start and was able to hurry back to her office to add the finishing touches to her story.

Twenty-five-year-old Joe had only been four years old when his mother drove him out to a remote spot in the desert. To have been rejected so cruelly caused a deep, persistent ache in Joe's heart and soul, a yearning, and loneliness, she thought. Ling's eyes welled up. She knew exactly what she needed to tack onto the end.

Even new babies recognize the voices of their mothers. They learn them in the womb and crave them all of their lives. As children, they know their mother's smell and will recognize it forever. Joe kept the blue blanket with his mother's scent that provides the hard evidence that he was her killer.

Our hearts must go out to all the abandoned children currently living in foster or adoptive homes and also to all the adults now living on their own with the forever pain of knowing their own biological mothers rejected them.

And how about all the children living in loveless, non-caring homes, emotionally abandoned by mothers who regard them as impediments to their freedom to do whatever, with whomever, whenever?

The supreme irony is that such mothers end up enslaved by their very own lifestyle choices.

By three forty-five that Monday afternoon, November 4, when most of the reporters were racing back to their computers after the long press conference with Sandingis, Ling took one last look at her story and, completely satisfied, pressed *Send.*

87

*L*ing entered her apartment at seven forty-five Monday night, kicked off her two-inch wedge slides and hugged Delphinium, who was faithfully waiting by the front door. It had been a gloriously long and fulfilling day.

"Delph, you must be starving," she said as she hurriedly filled the greyhound's food and water bowls.

Though Ling had only eaten a granola bar since breakfast, her level of excitement all day had obscured any hunger pangs. As she was about to search the fridge for an easy-fix meal, her phone rang.

Sandingis' tone of voice was jubilant.

"If there's ever a reason for both of us to celebrate, it's tonight."

Ling held her breath and waited for more.

"Ling, is it too late to ask you out for dinner?"

She was still pumped and full of adrenaline. Her voice climbed into its upper register. "I would love that."

"How's Vigilucci's sound?"

"Perfect."

"I'm out the door and on the way."

"I'll be ready. Just stop in for a quick second so Delph can meet you."

"Does Delph like meeting all the men in your life?"

Ling laughed, playing along. "You're the first one I'm going to introduce her to."

Ling slid back into her wedges and walked into the bathroom to freshen up. As she reapplied lipstick and blush, she flashed back to the first time she'd met the five foot eleven, trim, mild-mannered detective. It was at the crime scene and she had immediately felt a special connection.

During the time they had brainstormed and shared ideas for bringing down the killer, a mutual respect and trust kept building. Though no romantic interest had been outwardly expressed by either, she sensed an underlying attraction on his part. And she definitely was attracted to him. How could she ever forget that moment in his office when he turned around to walk back behind his desk and accidentally brushed very lightly alongside her.

Electric!

But, as always, she automatically dismissed any hint of such interest in her as ludicrous. Such a man deserves to have a magazine cover beauty at his side, she would tell herself.

She felt Delphinium's smooth fur brush up against her legs.

"The man of my dreams," she said, and then she heard his knock on the door.

88

The sun stretched and yawned, causing shafts of gold to light-speed across the ocean. The air was cool and crisp. Wispy cirrus clouds floated above without a care in the world. It was Saturday, November 9, exactly four weeks since Peggy's shocking discovery.

The SoCal Sleuths. That's how the media now referred to Peggy, Barb, and Cassie. In the five days since the jetty murder case had been solved, they were invited to appear on a couple of local TV shows, and Inside Edition set a date to shoot video next week of the threesome as they walked and talked along the beach.

Continuing messages on Twitter were about some aspect of the case. Peggy had to chuckle as she recalled a tweet sent by Millennial Mike, "These three ladies—older but not old— have got it going on!"

A lady in a one-shoulder-strap black swimsuit with a skirt caught Peggy's eye. There was no mistaking the woman's stage of life. Her white hair was pulled neatly back into a bun with a black wrap around it. Their glances met and the elderly woman smiled. There's no age limit to elegance and dignity, thought Peggy.

My guess is since she puts effort into her everyday appearance, she probably injects enthusiasm into all facets of life. Part of a favorite quote came to Peggy's mind: "…Grant that I may know that each age from first to last is good in itself and may be lived happily."

The full-throated laughter of her approaching friends startled a sandpiper and it scurried away. Peggy whirled around and gave them both a hug. "We're enjoying a good belly laugh about how jammed our schedules are," Barb explained. "What with our newfound notoriety, how on earth will we get everything done in time for Thanksgiving?"

"Are you expecting both your sons this year," asked Cassie.

"Sons, daughters-in-law, and the five grandchildren."

"Packed house," said Cassie. "My daughter's flying out from Pittsburgh with her two little girls but my med school son can't make it until Christmas. What about you, Peggy?"

"Our son, daughter-in-law, and 11-year-old granddaughter Annie are coming over. Mack's side of the family—his parents and brother— will arrive the day before Thanksgiving from Indiana."

As they began to walk in unison, Peggy could not hold back a wide smile. "Good thing we don't have any mysteries to solve at this particular time of year."

Cassie's voice evolved to super animated. "Wait. What? Are you saying you're open to solving another one?"

"Who knows what adventures lie ahead for us?

"After all, we're *The SoCal Sleuths*."

Epilogue

THREE MONTHS LATER

"**S**hhhh!" Peggy put a finger to her lips. "Here they come."

Mack thrust his hands out and waved them up and down, signaling Barb and Drew, Cassie and Nicholas, to hide in the kitchen.

As soon as the bell rang, Peggy and Mack, already in position, opened their front door wide.

"Congratulations on your engagement," Peggy smiled, stepping forward and hugging Ling while Mack heartily shook hands with Blane. "We're so excited for you both."

Realizing the four of them were standing outside, Peggy led the way into the living room. Mack gave his little prearranged cough. Nothing happened. Mack coughed louder and everyone practically flew out of the kitchen, all shouting *Surprise* and *Congratulations* at once.

Drew and Nicholas introduced themselves to Blane while the four women formed a hugging circle, all smiles, laughter, and good wishes for a long and wonderful marriage.

Cassie could not hold back. "All along, I knew you two were a match," she bragged. "You met under unusual circumstances. Nicholas and I did too. We bumped into each other while we were line dancing."

"We?" Nicholas grinned. "You mean it was your first time in the line dance class and you grapevined right into me."

"And we've been inseparable ever since," Cassie proudly pronounced.

Peggy gave a look to Barb and Cassie and they followed her into the kitchen. Within moments, they returned, carrying Osso Buco, Pasta Aglio e Olio with pinenuts, and asparagus tips. Mack poured the Pinot Noir.

"So you proposed last weekend?" Peggy asked Blane.

"It felt like forever waiting for the right time." His hand reached for Ling's and clasped it tightly.

Ling chuckled. "He waited until three publishers got in touch about my upcoming book on child abandonment. I was on top of the world."

"A woman's mood is of the utmost importance when proposing."

Everyone laughed heartily as they took their seats around Peggy and Mack's large, round Italian marble dinner table.

"Well, you've got three happily married couples here, and you two will be the fourth," added Barb, "to prove that marriages can be and are successful where there is true devotion, kindness, patience, and a sense of humor."

The End

Author's Notes

*P*eggy Crawford and her two friends were first introduced in my earlier book, *No Rocking Chairs Yet.* In this debut mystery novel, *Secret of the Jetty,* they don new hats and put their ingenuity and inventiveness to work to unearth a series of clues that will lead to the shocking solution of a mystery that attracts national attention.

Many thanks to dear friends and family members who kept cheering me on through daily life's countless interruptions and time-usurping challenges.

A special thank-you goes to Gretchen Ashton, who appeared as Peggy on the cover of my first book, for helping me to exhale during episodes of writer's block and also to Marie De Chantel for her support throughout this project.